BLOOD LESSONS

ORLANDO A. SANCHEZ

ABOUT THE STORY

The hardest lessons are taught in blood.

The power unleashed during the Ascendance, lingers. After defeating the Revenant, Monty realizes Simon's blood has been poisoned—tainted. Simon is slowly transforming. His body is harnessing dark magic in ways thought unimaginable.

Now, Monty is faced with the hardest choice, let the poison run its course, transforming Simon into a dark immortal, increasing his power, but drawing the attention of those who would want him dead, or allow Simon to take the blood lessons, risking his friend's life?

Can Monty help Simon before he's too far gone or will Simon become an unstoppable threat? Monty must act fast, before the power poisoning Simon's blood becomes too powerful to stop and eliminates them all.

ISBN: 9798359117289

QUOTATIONS

"You did thirst for blood, and with blood I fill you."
— Dante Alighieri

We few, we happy few, we band of brothers;
For he to-day that sheds his blood with me
Shall be my brother.
—William Shakespeare

ONE

Night descended on the city like a warm cloud.

I gazed out of the window into the coming night and winced as the pain in my body made its presence clear. I rolled up my sleeves and looked down at the veins in my arms in the dimming light. The deep violet-black lattice of power pulsed in rhythm with my heart, running up and down my forearms. The sight unnerving enough to guarantee that I wore long-sleeve shirts at all times.

I had been poisoned, and the poison was coursing through my body.

I felt it.

An odd presence that flowed through me: something alien, something other, something powerful and primal. I usually kept my eyes closed in the darkened room—partially to help me focus on dealing with the pain, mostly to keep from scaring the nurses into an early retirement.

Thanks to the ascendancy cast *and* my runic poisoning, along with whatever Orethe did to Ebonsoul, my eyes were now constantly glowing a deep red. I had my very own imitation of my hellhound's baleful glare, minus the beams shooting out of my eyes.

Despite my personal appreciation, my glowing eyes scared most of the staff attending me. You'd think that working in Haven, they'd be used to seeing glowing eyes.

Sunglasses didn't help; every pair I tried would eventually —usually in a matter of hours—disintegrate into its component parts. Outside of bandaging my eyes, there was no way of getting around the glow.

For some reason I couldn't explain, Roxanne had decided I needed to be in the normal wing of Haven, where glowing eyes and massive hellhounds were not the norm.

It explained the private room and reaction from the staff. All of them were reluctant to interact with me, except for the Head Nurse, Nan, who I guessed was part troll and all battle-axe.

Nan—short for Hanna I later learned, a name no one ever used on pain of being twisted into a human pretzel—was as pleasant as a crowbar to the face. Her usual dark mood caused the other nurses and doctors to avoid her when she was on the floor making her rounds.

She spoke in a series of disapproving grunts and nods, never saying more than one or two sentences in our brief interactions.

Nan reminded me of the old-style Soviet power-lifters, who bench-pressed trucks as a warm-up exercise. She towered over all of the nurses, male and female. An air of menace, like an impending natural disaster, announced her presence on the floor at least five minutes before she materialized.

By the time she actually arrived, every other nurse and most of the doctors had mysteriously discovered emergencies in other parts of Haven that needed their immediate attention, leaving Nan and her unlucky patient alone.

These days. one of those unlucky patients was me.

Tall and broad, she always wore her graying hair in a severe bun. My senses didn't pick up anything extra-normal about her, and to my knowledge she didn't carry any weapons, but I didn't dismiss the possibility.

Stranger things had happened in my life.

Monty carried his wailing blades in some kind of pocket dimension. It wasn't too farfetched that Nan would carry some type of weapon. Although, being in proximity to her, I realized her fists—which were nearly the size of my head— would make excellent weapons on their own.

We'd gotten into a routine. At the start of each evening she'd come in, take my vitals, make some notes on the chart, and act as if glowing red eyes and massive hellhounds were par for the course.

She was brave enough to pet Peaches on his massive head a few times, while tutting at me about the rules, and how dogs that big were not allowed on the hospital premises, even if I was friends with Director DeMarco.

Rules were rules.

Her daily interactions with Peaches were the only time a smile dared to cross her lips, vanishing immediately the moment she looked up at me. I seriously wondered who she had threatened to allow her to become a nurse; she seemed far better suited for a profession where pain was to be inflicted, not treated.

Even though she was sour enough to make lemons appear sweet, Peaches liked her, which meant she wasn't all bad. He was an excellent judge of character...unless meat was involved.

I glanced down at my chain-sawing hound as he napped and smiled.

No matter what they tried, there was no way they could remove him from my bedside. I was impressed when he refused to let himself be bribed by sausage. I thought for sure that would convince him, but all he did was eat the sausage and blink back into the room. After a few days of this, they gave up trying to remove him from my presence.

Pain lanced through my body, a hot poker of agony shoved in my chest, drawing my attention inward. I braced myself and focused my breathing, reaching internally for my weapon, Ebonsoul.

More searing pain bloomed throughout my body and mind, stealing my breath and making me gasp. Sweat formed on my brow as the pain clamped around the muscles in my midsection and squeezed unmercifully.

It had been a week since I had been admitted to Haven. The room I was in didn't compare to the palatial prison Roxanne had kept Monty in, not that I was complaining. Aside from being on the top floor of the normal wing and the privacy I'd been afforded, it looked like any other ordinary hospital room.

I shifted in the bed with a grunt of discomfort.

I could barely move, and the poison, along with the excruciating pain, had shown no signs of diminishing. I was beginning to wonder if Kali's curse had lost its ability to deal with the damage to my body.

Orethe's words came back to me: *It's only pain, Simon. You should be intimately acquainted with it by now.*

"Oh, we're acquainted, trust me," I grumbled under my breath after a few more gasps. "We're practically best friends by now."

"You're trying too hard," a voice said in the darkness. "You need to embrace the pain, work past it. Make the pain work for you."

Hades.

This was his second visit since my poisoning.

"Thanks for dropping by," I said, before clenching my teeth against the agony. "Just make the pain work for me, you say? Sounds easy enough. It's only mind-numbing, debilitating pain."

"Exactly," he replied. "Now you're beginning to understand."

I opened my eyes and fixed him with a glare.

"Why isn't my curse working against this pain?"

"What makes you think it isn't?"

That answer froze my thoughts.

"What?" I asked, confused. "You're saying...?"

"Your curse has arrested the poison, and is the only thing keeping you alive at this moment," he said calmly. "It's doing its job admirably."

If my curse was working—and I had no reason to believe it wasn't, aside from my constant agony—it meant that this pain had the potential to be much, much worse.

"How do I stop it?" I asked. "The pain. I need it to stop, at the very least, I needed it lessened or redirected."

"I told you," he said with a sigh. "You need to embrace it. Surrender to the pain. Pain is like any other sensation: cold, hot, tired, energized. It's merely a sensation your body is transmitting as a reaction to stimuli. In your case, the stimuli is internal."

"Ebonsoul?"

"That, and the runic poison, which is obstructing your access."

"The poison is blocking my access?" I asked, looking down at my arms. "That makes sense."

He nodded and pointed at me. It seemed that one of the perks of having a version of the baleful glare was excellent night vision. I saw him clearly as he reclined and stared at me.

"Materialize your weapon."

"I'm getting off the agony express for today," I said, laying my head back in my pillow. "It doesn't want—"

"*It* doesn't?"

"Figure of speech," I said, raising a hand quickly. "No, it's not sentient or speaking to me. It's just not forming when I want it to. I keep trying, but it's like trying to grab smoke."

"You don't want *that* blade to become sentient," he said. "*I* don't want that blade to become sentient, especially not now, after Orethe's...improvements. did. In fact, to be on the safe side, make sure you and the Night Warden avoid being close to each other until you have your weapon under your control."

"What happens if I get too close to his weapon?" I asked. "Do we explode?"

Hades fixed me with a glare, then looked to the side before answering.

"At least you have maintained your special brand of humor," he said. "You should be concerned. This is the worst case of runic poisoning I've ever seen while the subject was still alive."

"Now I feel special," I said, staring at him. "You don't know how to fix this?"

"Outside of ending your life?"

"I'm a big fan of the 'continuing to live' club, thanks. Yes, without erasing me from existence."

"Not really, but I am interested in how this will play out," he said. "Evidently, you're in no danger of dying, or you'd be a corpse by now. This is unexplored territory."

"Great, I'm the Magellan of poisoning," I answered with a scowl. "Isn't Grey the one person I should be speaking to? Doesn't he have a similar condition too?"

"He would have no insight for you," Hades said, his voice dark. "His condition stems from a cast that exceeded his capacity at the time. His body rebelled, and the backlash should have killed him—it *was* killing him, until he bonded with the sword."

"Sounds sort of like what happened to me."

"His condition differs from yours considerably," Hades said with a small shake of his head. "He's not being kept alive by a curse. He is in a symbiotic relationship with a voracious, powerful, and bloodthirsty goddess who resides in his sword."

"That's why you want me to keep Ebonsoul away from him?"

"The two weapons are a set," he said. "I thought you knew how much or if any of her essence was placed within your weapon. For now, your weapon seems to be dormant."

"You think getting close will wake up Ebonsoul?"

"I don't know," Hades said, pensively. "Right now, I don't wish to find out, and neither do you. Now, stop stalling and form your blade."

I sat up again and focused.

"I'm not stalling," I said. "I'm just not in the mood for the wonderful side effect sensation of the pickaxe being forced into my ear repeatedly. That's all."

"Stop being so dramatic," Hades replied. "You're bonded to a hellhound, while being the cursed immortal—Marked of Kali, *and* the Aspis to a Mage Montague—no small thing, I might add. You're also the wielder of Ebonsoul, in no small part due to your bond with a certain ancient vampire, a seraph, and now necromantic weapon, thanks to Orethe. I would think the small price of a little agony comes with the territory, don't you?"

"No, I don't think it should come with the territory," I snapped. "Actually, I'd prefer an agony-free life, thank you very much. This isn't even remotely fair. I'd at least like the option of sharing my agony with others."

He gave me a small smile as he shook his head.

"It's too late for that, Strong," he said. "I never said any of this was fair. Life isn't fair. Anyone who says differently is selling you something, or trying to exploit you."

"Tell me about it. I didn't ask for any of this."

"Some are born great, some achieve greatness, and some have greatness thrust upon them," Hades said. "I would say you fall squarely into the latter category."

"Did you just Bard me?"

"I did," Hades replied, growing serious. "How long have you been here? In Haven?"

"About a week, why?"

He nodded his head slowly.

"That tracks," he said, "especially with the heightened Verity activity."

"*What* heightened Verity activity?"

"You need to understand that machinations are being formed as you squander your time here," he said, waving a hand. "Instead of doing what's necessary, you dwell on the trifling matter of a little pain and discomfort. What you are experiencing now will pale in comparison to what is headed your way if you don't, as you say, suck it up and get it done."

"Excuse me?" I said. "What are you talking about?"

"Even now, as we speak, Verity is assembling a task force to destroy you, Tristan, and your hellhound," he explained. "How long do you think it will be before they breach the robust defenses of Haven?"

That was why Roxanne had me in the normal wing. She was hiding me in plain sight. Even as strong as the defenses were at Haven, they couldn't hold out indefinitely. Having me here was putting everyone at risk.

"Not long enough," I said. "I seem to recall Verity having no consideration for collateral damage."

"Can you imagine how many will die because you failed to grasp the severity of your situation and chose to wallow in your *pain*?" he asked. "I'm sure they will accept your apology for being too weak to face what you can't escape, as they perish by the hundreds."

"You're laying it on a little thick there," I said, annoyed. "I get it. I need to get off my ass and start these blood lessons, whatever they are."

"You do," he agreed. "You start by forming your blade."

"Shit. Somehow I knew you were going to say that."

"Do you need motivation? I'm sure I could summon a creature to threaten the patients here, which would force you into action."

"No help needed, thanks," I said, heavily. "I have plenty of motivation."

"It doesn't appear to be the case," he said. "I'd like to see you prove me wrong."

"You can be a cold bastard."

"The absolute coldest," he said, tapping the top of his wrist with a finger. "Tempus fugit."

I closed my eyes and focused again. The pain was there, but washing over it was the anger and frustration. The unfairness of being put in this position, the anger at being targeted by more enemies than I cared to count at the moment; the barely controlled rage at being a pawn to beings more powerful than I could ever hope to be, moving along a plan at their whim, without control or agency.

"I really hate gods and their games," I said, seething. "Present company semi-included."

"I know," Hades said. "If you want to stop us from playing with you, stop us from using you as a pawn, then you need to grow stronger—stronger than you are now, stronger than you can imagine. Strong enough to make us respect you and perceive you as a threat. This is the first step. Form. Your. Blade."

I reached inside for Ebonsoul. It burned as I wrapped my mind and intention around it. Through the fiery sensation that suddenly engulfed me, I materialized the silver mist. It was still mainly silver, but had violet streaks and sections of yellow swirling throughout.

The pain nearly blinded me.

I didn't stop to give it much thought as I willed my blade into a solid form. It materialized in my hand, a heavy weight of power and death. The black blade gleamed with power as the runes pulsed red, violet and gold.

That's new.

"There," I said, holding up Ebonsoul. "Happy?"

"Ecstatic," Hades said, fading away. "Imagine how overjoyed the Verity agents approaching this floor will be when they see that weapon in your hand as they come through that door."

"You're not serious," I said, jumping out of bed and reabsorbing Ebonsoul with little discomfort. "They're inside Haven? Where's Roxanne? Monty?"

"Otherwise occupied, I'm afraid," he said. "The safety of all these lives depend on you and your hound. I have full faith in your abilities. Nan will buy you time to compose yourself and help you exit. Get dressed and get moving."

"Nan will what?" I asked, confused. "What are you talking about?"

Hades had disappeared.

I heard the shouts in the distance, followed by screams of terror.

Nan stepped into my room wearing combat armor, locking the door behind her and holding a large, double-bladed axe that looked nearly as scary as Nemain.

A battle-axe.

One covered in dark energy.

She had also grown at least a foot since I last saw her earlier in the day. She gazed down at me, giving me a curt nod.

"You make one comment about me and Stormchaser here, and you won't have to worry about the Verity agents headed this way," she said, giving me a once over. "Get dressed. We don't have much time."

TWO

"Let me guess, you're not really a nurse?" I asked, getting dressed as fast as possible. "At least not a nurse in any conventional sense."

"Why would you say that?" she said as she focused on the door.

"Oh, I don't know, the axe covered in black energy, the combat armor, the fact that you're about a foot taller now and radiating a major energy signature?" I said, looking at the door. "Those seem like strong clues."

"Focus on putting on your clothes, not on my occupation," she snapped. "For your information, I'm an excellent combat medic, quite capable of reinserting your intestines and making sure you can continue fighting if need be."

"That fills me with all kinds of confidence," I grumbled as I got dressed. "Can we handle what's coming?"

Peaches padded over to where I stood and rumbled as Nan glanced at me and nodded.

"I have stood on and survived battlefields that would make you weep in despair," she said, glancing at my hellhound. "Spilled rivers of blood deep enough to drown in.

Facing a bunch of jumped-up mages after a child immortal, is practically insulting. I can see why I'm the only one here."

"I'm going to take that as a yes," I said, examining her armor, which seemed vaguely familiar. "You wouldn't happen to know a group of Valkyries known as the Nightwing, would you?"

"You're sharp," she said, giving me a look. "I am the tip of the spear that is the Midnight Echelon."

"Where are your wings?" I asked against all sense of self-preservation. "Don't all Valkyries have wings?"

"I was instructed to blend in with the normals," she said. "Wings are not suitable for blending in."

"Good point," I said, looking around. "Can't we just find another exit?"

She looked at the windows and shook her head.

"One way in and one way out," she said. "Easy to defend, difficult to escape. We'll have to make a new exit."

"Making a new exit sounds painful," I said with a wince. "Why not just use a window?"

"You're welcome to try," she said. "The sorceress has made sure to protect this room." She pointed at the windows. "See for yourself."

I used my innersight and cautiously gazed at the window. Each pane erupted in a runic combination of golds and reds with accents of violets here and there.

Runes covered the windows, walls, ceiling and floor. The door had runes, but nowhere near the amount on the other surfaces in the room.

"This room is covered in runic defenses," I said with surprise. "How exactly do you intend to make a new exit?"

"Patience. We'll have help from your friend outside."

Her explanation made no sense. All of my friends were forbidden from visiting me. With the exception of Monty and Peaches, no one was allowed to come to my room.

"That doesn't remotely make sense," I said, examining the runes again. "I can't make out most of those runes."

"The sorceress has used some potent magic," she said. "My presence here means some consider you worth protecting, though I don't know the threat you pose, despite your titles."

"Thanks. Really. Roxanne doesn't fool around with the security," I said, turning my gaze away before I got a migraine. "Do you prefer to be called Nan or do you have some Midnight Echelon call sign?"

She gave me a look of mild disapproval.

"My given name is Hanna, but *you* may call me Nan," she said, hefting her axe. "My true name will not be shared."

"Fair enough," I said. "I can respect that. My name is—"

"Strong," she finished. "Simon Strong. I know who you are. Bondmate to the Mighty Peaches, scion of the Guardian to the Underworld, Cerberus, who is the bondmate to Hades, Lord of the Underworld, and ally to the All-Father, my lord."

Somehow it felt like I was the footnote in that sentence.

"Why would Verity be coming for me?" I wondered aloud. "I'm not a mage. Like you said, I'm not much of a threat."

"Wrong," she said. "I said I didn't *see* the threat you posed. I never said you weren't a threat. If we were enemies, and I had to choose between you and Mage Montague, I would dispatch you first."

"No need to rub it in," I said, annoyed. "I get it. He's a mage and wields phenomenal cosmic power. I'm not, and I don't. It's not like—"

"You misunderstand," she said, cutting me off. "You're a cursed immortal, bonded to a purebred hellhound and a Mage Montague. You are the Marked of Kali, wielding a seraphic weapon of death. In my eyes, you are the greater threat. I would attempt to kill you first. It is a status worthy of respect."

She knew entirely too much about me.

"How exactly do you know—?"

"Cain is still alive," she added. "He may be neutralized for now, but he should have been removed from the board. It's what I would have done."

"I tend to agree," I said. "Leaving enemies alive is only inviting future problems."

Nan nodded.

"By leaving an enemy alive, you've only delayed the inevitable. Cain will not stop, and his second, in Verity, Tana, will not rest until she has eliminated you and Mage Montague. There is a reason why even among the Blades, they call her the Bloody Dagger with fear upon their lips."

"Removing Cain wasn't my call to make," I said. "He was stripped of power."

"Stripped of his personal power, yes. Influence? No. He still leads the Blades; only now, Tana acts as his fist when violence is needed."

"So we replaced Cain with Tana," I said. "That sounds bad."

"Because it is," Nan said. "She is a ruthless zealot when it comes to Verity and its tenets, possessing the power to enforce them."

"Is there any—?"

A thunderous crash slammed into the door, caving it in. The door bowed inward, but held, barely. Outside the door, a roar threatened to deafen all of the patients on the level.

"That sounds like a worthy challenge," Nan said with a wide smile. "Gird yourself, Strong, and live up to your name. Do you have your weapon?"

"I do," I said, with a tap of Grim Whisper in my holster. "Entropy rounds should slow that thing down."

She looked at Grim Whisper, raised an eyebrow, and then

looked back at me as if I had described advanced cotton balls of destruction.

"*That* is not a weapon," she said, looking at my holster before narrowing her eyes and looking at me. "Ready your true weapon." She pointed at my chest. "The one you carry within."

"That might not be a good idea," I said, trying to avoid forming Ebonsoul again. "It's a little difficult to summon right now, not to mention painful, and too dangerous."

"Too dangerous and painful, you say?"

"I do," I replied. "It's loaded with all kinds of death castings that I may not be able to control yet. Using it right now would be a bad idea."

"You fear that your weapon may be *too* deadly?" she asked incredulously. "What do you intend to do, then, beguile them with your words as they try to take your life?"

"Monty says it's always best to use tact and diplomacy."

"Is that what he does before he unleashes the destruction?"

"We try," I admitted. "Hasn't really worked up to this point."

"It has been noticed," she said. "It will be hard to use tact and diplomacy with an enemy trying to rip your arms and legs off, don't you think?"

"It's not like Verity is going to send an ogre," I said with a half chuckle. "They're mages, *human* mages, not devastating creatures of destruction."

"Of course they are," she agreed. "I can, however, assure you, that the creature on the other side of this door is most certainly not a human mage."

Another roar filled the corridor, followed by the pounding of some kind of battering ram on the door. This time the door didn't hold, and buckled inward, revealing a living nightmare.

A hideous face peered in through the gap of the door and the frame. One large, yellow eye, attached to a monstrosity of a face, looked around until it focused on me.

It was an ogre.

"Strong," it hissed. "Mine."

THREE

"That's an ogre," I said, taking a few steps back as the face disappeared from view. "Verity sent an ogre?"

"Your powers of perception are truly staggering," Nan said, pushing the door back into the frame. "That door will not withstand another attack. The runic seal has been broken."

I looked at the mangled door, surprised it was still attached to the door frame, and had to agree. One strong blow would send it flying.

"How exactly are we going to leave the room?" I asked. "I mean, without going through an angry ogre."

"There is no other kind of ogre," she said, glancing around the room, settling her gaze on the wall closest to us. "We go through there."

"Through the rune-covered wall?" I asked incredulously. "The very solid-looking rune-covered wall?"

"We will use the creature to create our new exit," she replied. "Ready your weapon. Now."

I materialized Ebonsoul with a low grunt of pain, nearly

losing my balance as the agony gripped me. Nan placed a massive hand on my shoulder, steadying me.

"I'm good," I said, raising a hand and feeling anything but. "You plan on us facing that thing head-on?"

"Not us, me. You are going to weaken that wall," she said, pointing to a wall next to the window. "Once the creature destroys the door, you bury your blade in the wall."

"You realize we're on the top floor?" I asked, glancing out of the window. "It's an easy ten stories."

"Fifteen on this side of Haven," she corrected me, as if that made things better. "Do you fear heights?"

"It's not the height, exactly," I explained, still looking out at the street below. "It's the falling from them that I like to avoid."

"Perhaps you can explain that to the ogre? It may let you pass. More likely it will try to crush your skull as soon as you get close. Would you like to try?"

I seriously doubted having a conversation with an ogre could end any way but painfully, no matter how intelligent it was. I shook my head, looking for another alternative that didn't require absorbing immense amounts of energy into my poisoned body.

"My weapon is a siphon," I warned. "The backlash could—"

"What? Kill you? I doubt it," she finished. "In any case, that is our new exit. Your siphon will weaken the wall just enough."

"We're not going to fight the ogre?"

"I certainly could, but my instructions were to keep you secure," she said. "Verity has sent more than one of these creatures to apprehend you."

"Apprehend?" I asked. "Not kill?"

"I'm sure that's on the list," she said with another tight smile. "But taking you alive ensures Mage Montague gives chase. They want him dead, which means they take you alive...for now."

"I thought I was the greater threat?"

"Yes, but you are not the mage they want to kill," she corrected. "To them, you are a means to an end. It's flattering, if you think about it."

"Somehow, 'flattering' is not the first word that comes to mind."

"Regardless, you are not capable of fighting this creature in your condition. Facing it in combat would put you in mortal danger. We must—"

"Engage in a tactical retreat?" I finished. "I have some skill in those. I'm almost a tactical retreat master at this point."

She gave me a look and shook her head.

"Precisely, but first, we will send a message to buy us some time."

Another roar filled the corridor outside the room as Nan stepped back, pushing me to the side, next to the wall she wanted weakened. The door blasted inward a second later, narrowly missing us both.

"Strong," the ogre said with a low growl. "Surrender and die."

"Isn't that supposed to be surrender *or* die?"

It responded with the sound of rocks being crushed by a sledgehammer, which I assumed was laughter.

"Surrender...*and* die."

I saw the intelligence behind the eyes, and realized this was no ordinary creature bent on mindlessly ripping my arms off. This was an intelligent monster, who would *mindfully* rip my arms off and attempt to beat me to death with them.

"Hideous and intelligent," I said. "I liked them more when they were just hideous."

"The wall," Nan said, stepping in front of the ogre. "Diplomacy is finished. Do it."

I plunged Ebonsoul into the wall as Nan unleashed a fist into the ogre's face, causing it to stumble back a few steps into the hallway. The runes in the wall exploded with violet light as my blade siphoned their power.

My blade disappeared a second later as the runes in the wall diminished in intensity, vanishing from sight. Almost immediately, the power from the defensive runes rushed into me, setting off a raging inferno of energy in my body.

I looked down at my body, half expecting to be blazing with runic fire as I burned inside. Peaches moved to my side, positioning himself between me and the doorway as I fell to one knee, holding onto his neck for balance.

It was getting harder to breathe, my breath coming in ragged, wheezing gasps.

<Should I lick you?>

<I'm not hurt. It's just hard to breathe.>

<Are you sure? You fell down. My saliva can heal you.>

<Power...too much power...coming from the runes.>

<If you ate more meat, the power wouldn't hurt you.>

I nearly burst into laughter—because his logic, as insane as it sounded, made perfect sense...to him. I also realized that my response meant my brain was melting as the power of the defensive runes flowed through me.

I needed to release some of the power I held.

I needed a target.

I extended a hand and aimed at the ogre.

"*Ignis...ignis vi*—!" I yelled as the power overwhelmed me. "Nan, down!"

A beam of violet energy shot out from my hand, headed for the ogre.

Nan dropped to the floor as the beam seared the air above her. It punched into the ogre's chest, lifting it off its feet and slamming it into the wall at the end of the short corridor behind it.

The ogre shook its head as it roared in pain. It glared at me for a few seconds, then started running in my direction, leaping over the prone Nan as it focused on me.

"Well, shit," I muttered, gripping Peaches' neck as my vision tunneled. "That wasn't nearly as effective as I expected."

Peaches let out a low growl and stepped into "crush and rend" mode as the ogre bore down on us. Nan had jumped to her feet, catching up to the ogre as it entered the room.

She reached out and grabbed the ogre by the arm as she pivoted, twisting the ogre off its intended path of my imminent stomping and through the wall Ebonsoul had weakened.

It was like watching a moment of aggressive ogre shot-putting as she rotated and launched the ogre through the wall, out of Haven, and into the street below. The ogre landed on the street below with a sick crunch. Nan looked down and glanced back at me, then looked down at the street again.

"Huh," she said, pensively. "I thought it would be able to withstand a fall from this height. Was that your magic missile?"

"Yes. Wait, how did you know I call it a magic—"

"It must possess some kind of weakening effect," she said. "Ogres are very resilient creatures. It usually takes more than a fall, even from this height, to finish one of their kind. That ogre should have survived."

"You are incredibly well-informed about me," I said, warily. "How do you know all of this?"

"The Midnight Echelon is tasked to monitor and deal with threats, as is all of the Nightwing," she said. "Any threat of import is investigated and kept under surveillance in case neutralization is required."

"You've been keeping tabs on me?" I asked, looking out of

the ogre-sized hole in the wall and into the night. "Watching me?"

"Yes. You, Mage Montague, and the Mighty Peaches are dangerous individually, but together? Together, you pose a significant threat. One worth watching."

"In case we need to be neutralized?"

Her face darkened for a moment before she continued.

"Yes. It would bring me no pleasure," she said. "But if any of you turned to darkness, the Midnight Echelon would stand against you...and eliminate you."

Monty and I had faced a few heavy hitters in the past that had tried to do the same thing. She wasn't bragging; her answer was simply a statement of fact as she believed it.

The Midnight Echelon would stand against us, that was certain. As for eliminating us, that would be much harder than they imagined, not that I wanted to test out the theory while I had Verity after me.

"I have no intentions of stepping over to the dark side."

She nodded.

"Some choose evil, some have evil thrust upon them, and a very few are made to be so," she said, looking down at the ogre as another roar filled the hallway. "We need to go."

"I may be immortal, but that doesn't mean I'm immune to pain," I said, following her gaze to the ogre smashed on the street below. "Last time I checked, I don't fly."

"Well, the Mighty Peaches can plane-walk," she said, glancing down the hallway again before looking at my hound. "He will be a good hound and follow you wherever you go. Yes?" Peaches gave her a low rumble followed by some chuffing. "As for you, we will take a more direct route."

"A more direct—?"

She grabbed me by the waist and stepped out of the ogre-sized hole.

FOUR

The ground rushed up at us as we fell, and I screamed.

She smiled as she popped her wings halfway down, slowing our descent and gliding away from Haven. Her black wings blended into the night, making them nearly impossible to see.

"I'm glad you're enjoying yourself," I said, making an effort to remain still. "A little warning would've been nice."

"You did ask about my wings," she said as we landed on 1st Avenue and 26th Street, a few blocks away from Haven. "Now you've seen them."

"I could see how they would make it hard to blend in," I said, looking at her impressive wingspan. "I hope you'll understand if I don't want to see them this way ever again, thanks."

"That was a very courageous battle cry as we fell," she said as her wings faded from view. "Do you always scream when frightened?"

I shot a glare at her.

"I wasn't frightened," I said, defensively. "You just took

me by surprise. I don't usually make a habit of leaping off tall buildings in a single bound."

"Ah, *surprised*," she said, with a small smile. "That would explain the high-pitched wailing."

"There was no high-pitched anything," I countered. "I just didn't expect to use the newly created ogre exit as a way to escape."

Roars filled the night behind us, coming from Haven.

"We need to keep moving," she said, turning to look at Haven. "They won't stop pursuit unless we stop them, permanently."

"What about Haven?"

"What about it?"

"The people? You know, the innocent patients in the normal wing? Ogres running loose? Any of that ring a bell?"

"No one is innocent, Strong. Except, perhaps, for young children," she said. "The bulk of the Detention Facility is being secured by several members of the Ten. LD and TK are assisting the Director while we lead the threat away."

"What about the actual normal wing?" I asked. "They're still vulnerable. The Detention Facility is underground."

"The top three floors of the normal wing have been evacuated for more than a day," she said matter-of-factly. "The rest of the wing has been secured by the Director, her security force, and Mage Montague. You were the only person on that floor once we received warning of the approaching attack. Does that knowledge put you at ease?"

"At ease?" I said, getting angry. "You deliberately put me on the top floor to spring a trap?"

"Yes," she said, "even though it was not my idea."

"You *knew* about the attack?" I asked, confused. "No one thought it would've been a good idea to move the actual target of the attack? You know, for his safety? Instead of using me as bait?"

"No," she answered flatly, as she started moving fast. "That would give the impression we knew about the attack beforehand. It would compromise our people inside Verity."

"You have people inside Verity?" I asked as I came to a stop. Partially it was the shock of knowing Valkyries had infiltrated Verity; the other more pressing reason was because my lungs were on fire and running was becoming harder by the second. "I need a moment."

Peaches materialized next to me with a low rumble.

<More big creatures are coming. They smell bad.>

"This would not be a good time to stop and discuss the plan," she answered as she stopped and looked behind me. "Did I forget to mention they will give chase?"

"Are you saying it was decided to put my life in danger to protect your Valkyrie assets?" I asked, ignoring her. "Who thought *that* was a good idea?"

"Vi did," she said. "For the record, your life was *never* in danger."

"Verity sent two ogres after me," I said, raising my voice. "Two ogres is not risking my life?"

"Three, actually, and no, it wasn't, because *I* was there to make sure you made it out of the facility intact," she said, looking down at me. "That was and is my purpose. Are you currently intact?"

"Yes, I am."

"Would you like to remain that way? Or would you prefer we continue this conversation as the ogres tasked with capturing you, arrive?"

"Not a fan of ogres getting their hands on me no," I admitted begrudgingly. "I still would've appreciated knowing."

"Why?" she asked. "It wouldn't have changed the outcome. The ogres were, and are, still coming for you. This way, we maintain the flow of information out of Verity and the appearance of ignorance. This is the best possible outcome in my opinion."

"The best possible outcome would be not being chased by Verity," I said. "That would be the best possible outcome."

"I'm afraid that is impossible," she said, moving again as I tried to keep pace. "The use of a lost rune, a lost elder blood rune, is a significant transgression to the High Tribunal. I'm surprised Verity only unleashed ogres."

I stared at her.

At this point, I had accepted the fact that the Midnight Echelon had one of the best information-gathering techniques in the supernatural world. They were like the NSA, CIA, FBI and any other three-letter agency all wrapped into one entity.

"You're kidding, right?"

"I've seen and dispensed too much death, Strong. Humor is lost on me," she said, moving faster than anyone her size had a right to move. "I imagine Verity doesn't find any humor in this situation either. They have a tendency to be on the extreme side of things regarding rules and magic."

"It's a figure...figure of speech," I panted, doing my best to keep up with her and failing. "I need to slow down again for a second."

"Soon," she said, looking down the street. "Only a little farther, and then you can stop. This too, has been planned for."

"Where exactly are we going?"

"We need to get you to the water," she said. "23rd Street leads to the East River. There, Mage Montague will be waiting to take you off the island, at least until the ogres are dealt with."

I looked down the street. We were still a few blocks from 23rd, and to get to the river we had one long block to run. The ogres would intercept us by then.

"The ogres will catch up to us before we hit the river," I said as the roars behind us increased in volume. "We should stop and fight."

"Yes and no."

"What?" I said. "I'm not in the mood to run and die tired. We should stop here and fight them."

"You really aren't good at listening, are you?" she said, whirling on me as she came to a stop and pointed a finger at my chest. "*You* can't fight while poisoned. Your condition makes you a danger, not only to yourself, but to everyone around you. Is any part of what I am saying unclear to you?"

"I understand the words, but I'm not getting why I'm a danger," I said, risking a gentle tap by her enormous fist. "I formed Ebonsoul and weakened the wall. I can face an ogre."

She stared at me for a few seconds before shaking her head.

"I truly do not understand how you are still alive."

"I hear that often," I said. "It's a gift."

"A gift like that can get you killed if you are not careful."

"Heard that, too," I said. "Can you clarify why we don't just pound these ogres?"

"No, I can't," she said. "Yes, they will intercept us—that's part of the plan and the reason we are not *flying* to the river. *I* will slow them down while *you* reach the river. We do not deviate from this plan, understood?"

"Understood," I said, giving it some thought. "This is *not* a great plan."

"Plans are worthless, but planning is everything," she said. "Good plans are designed to be malleable. Great plans are a fantasy. Keep moving."

She took off running again and kept going until we reached 23rd Street. On the corner of 23rd and 1st Avenue, she formed her battle axe and slammed it into the street, burying the blade in the soft asphalt.

"What are you doing?"

"Stick to the plan, Strong," she said. "It has been an honor. Now follow this street"—she pointed down 23rd Street—"until you reach the river. Do not turn back, no matter what you see or hear."

"You're going to face off against two ogres? Alone?"

"It's *only* two ogres," she said, rolling her shoulders and cracking her neck. "Mage Montague and the others are expecting you. Don't keep them waiting. Verity will send more of their people soon. This is merely a stopgap measure; something to distract them while you deal with your condition."

A roar followed by several more filled the night.

"Are you sure you can handle this?" I asked, looking into the night. "That sounds like more than two ogres."

She grabbed the hilt of the battle axe and looked down at me with a grin.

"I really hope so," she said. "Get going. Stormchaser's energy signature will attract them to my location, but not for long. Your energy signature is difficult to mask or diffuse. If you remain here, they will find you. This is why you must head to the river."

"What do you—"

"Now, Strong. Go."

She removed the axe from the street and whirled it around a few times before stepping into a defensive stance. The black energy around its blades wafted off its surface, streaming into the night.

"Thank you," I said. "For everything. Well, everything except the short flight to the street."

"It was my duty," she said, without looking at me. "I expect you to possess a more manly battle cry when we next meet."

I was about to answer when another roar, much closer

than before, drowned out my thoughts. I looked down at Peaches and rubbed his head. He rumbled at me in response, followed by a low growl.

"Time to go," I said, and headed down 23rd Street at a run with my hellhound by my side.

FIVE

I ran east down 23rd Street until I reached the river.

Peaches, who could've easily left me behind, kept pace with me, because he was amazing that way. Halfway down the block, a sensation of charged energy crawled over my skin, causing me to slow down.

Peaches let out a low growl and stopped, looking behind us.

<What is it, boy?>

<The big lady is hitting the bad-smelling creatures.>

I turned to see a bolt of black energy race across the sky and hit the ground where I had left Nan. The bolt was followed by a thunderclap that sounded like several buildings had been demolished at once.

I really hope she isn't destroying buildings.

Loud roars and screams followed a few seconds after the thunderclap. This was soon followed by the sound of menacing laughter.

This wasn't infectious laughter that invited you to join in and share. No, this was the kind of laughter that chilled your blood—because you knew it was probably going to be the last sound you heard before your life was ripped from you.

It was the kind of laughter that invited pain and death.

I realized in that moment that all my ideas about Valkyries had been shaped by stories and myth. Meeting the Midnight Echelon had radically revised the concept of Valkyries in my mind into some kind of special black ops team of death and devastation.

Sounds like Nan is enjoying herself.

"Let's go, boy," I said, out loud, turning and running to the river as fast as my body allowed. "That's not our fight."

Five minutes later, I stood at the end of the deserted Skyport Marina, looking across the river at the towering shadows that was the ever growing skyline of West Queens.

It would never, could never, compete with the iconic skyline of Manhattan, but they were giving it their best shot. The river was a dark, flowing barrier filled with a primal deep energy of its own.

I've never sensed the energy of the river like this before.

I remembered something about how flowing water impacted the ability of magic users, making it difficult to cast. It was something Monty had shared some time ago, but I never made sense of it. I wondered if that was the reason so many places of power were islands, to contain the energy found on the island.

My senses picked up a feeling of nothingness, a moving void approaching my position as I looked into the night.

A boat sidled up to the marina near where I stood, giving me serious B-2 stealth bomber vibes. To call it a boat would be the same as calling the Dark Goat a car. This vessel was in a class by itself—even in the dark, I recognized the sleek lines of the Lamborghini Tecnomar 63 yacht.

Cecil was insane.

The cost of the yacht alone was an easy seven figures. The

fact that this vessel had been runed to within an inch of its life probably raised the figure into the stratosphere.

This superyacht was designed in the same spirit as the automobiles bearing the same brand. The emphasis was focused on style and speed. Mostly speed. Definitely speed. I doubted Ferruccio had something like this in mind when he set out to prove Ferrari wrong.

It was beyond impressive and covered in enough runes to make me think it was almost as indestructible as the Dark Goat. The black-and-red-accented yacht sidled up close to the marina, allowing me to read the name in the dim lights: *Mobula.*

It docked close enough for me to see Monty standing in the rear and speaking to someone I couldn't make out, due to being blocked by his body. I recognized Robert sitting in the pilot's seat.

The runes on the *Mobula's* surface fluctuated between orange and red, pulsing to a slow rhythm of their own and giving off a major energy signature that rivaled the Dark Goat's "keep away" runes.

Cecil had outdone himself with this yacht, which made me wonder about the bond between Cecil and Monty. Just how far back did their families go? Even when he did explain, he was a little light on the details.

Why did Cecil keep loaning these massively expensive vehicles to Monty, only to have them returned as abstract art? The bond between them ran deeper than I could understand.

"Do you intend to admire the yacht all night?" Monty asked, staring at me. "We do have places to go."

I shook myself out of my thoughts and stepped onboard the yacht. I stepped close to where they stood as Peaches chuffed, having found a comfy corner, turned in a circle a few times, and proceeded to sprawl, conquering part of the yacht as his domain.

The snoring followed soon after.

I shook my head at him and focused on Monty.

"Cecil has yachts now?" I asked, impressed as I took in the interior. "Since when?"

"If it's designed to transport goods or people, I expect Cecil to have SuNaTran involved in some way or another," Monty said, then turned to the person at his side. "I'm still somewhat surprised he actually built the Shrike. He is, in his own way, a genius of transportation."

"Does this mean he forgave you for your renovations of the Duesenberg?"

"*I* did not renovate it," Monty said. "That was *your* associate, Douglas, who decided to land on the automobile, rendering it to its component parts."

"I really hope *that* wasn't the excuse you gave Cecil," I said. "Douglas was not my associate. He was an insane, power-hungry nutcase with delusions of grandeur. Cecil already holds the Aventador against me, even though I had nothing to do with that one either. Tell me you didn't say Douglas was my friend or associate."

"Of course not," Monty said. "I explained that it was the handiwork of a deranged individual bent on destroying us. He seemed unimpressed. Something to the effect of, 'What else is new?'"

"Could be because there's been plenty of that going around these days," I said. "He must've been okay to lend you this beauty."

I ran a hand along the edge of the yacht, admiring its sleek lines.

"Cecil and I will *always* be okay," Monty answered after some thought. "Our families' history is too old and interconnected to allow material things to drive a wedge between us. The bond between the Montagues and Fairchilds—his family —goes back centuries. We were fighting, dying, side by side on bloody battlefields for as long as there have been wars between men."

"He said as much," I said. "Still doesn't explain why he loans you these insanely expensive vehicles."

"Back when I was a child, and my uncle Dex was considerably more...reckless, he saved Cecil's family," Monty answered after some thought. "We don't speak of it, ever. I'm surprised he shared that much with you. Without the Montagues, there would be no Fairchilds. It's that simple and that complicated."

"Basically, a debt that can never be repaid?"

"Indeed," Monty said with a nod. "My family's end of the obligation is to leverage the considerable fortune that has been amassed over the centuries to keep SuNaTran solvent."

"Are you part of SuNaTran?"

"Not an active part," he said. "We would be the equivalent of a silent partner. No one knows of our involvement in the company. We prefer to keep it that way."

"Well, that explains why he would lend you the vehicles he does," I said.

"I do try not to abuse the privilege," Monty added. "I have recently commissioned two Duesenberg models to be built. He is beside himself with glee."

"Two of them?"

"One to store and keep out of harm's way, the other to use in a limited fashion for some of his more...*distinguished* clients."

"No wonder he lent you this yacht," I said, looking around. "Two Duezys must have exploded his brain."

"I'm certain his brain will recover," he said, stepping to the side and gesturing to the person standing next to him. "I believe you remember Mage Quan of the White Phoenix?"

I nodded.

Quan still looked the same as I remembered. She wore a

long coat over a black silk robe, while an intricate tattoo of interwoven designs covered the top of her bare head and half her face.

The design gave off a soft turquoise glow, which was clear to my innersight. A simple, black robe tied at the waist with a white sash covered her slight frame.

The sash was interlinked with metal sections which blended into the tail of a white phoenix. The design snaked itself around her waist, up one shoulder and across her chest.

"The last time I saw her, we were dealing with Slif, Davros, and the werewolves," I said with a shudder as the memory resurfaced. "Hello, Quan."

"Hello, Simon," she said with a short bow. "It has been some time. Tris tells me you've grown in power since we last met."

I gave her a short bow in return and smiled at the nickname she had for Monty, who rolled his eyes at me, knowing I wouldn't let it go.

"Well, *Tris* has been reaching new heights too," I said. "Did he tell you?"

"No need," she said, her voice somber. "I can see the effects of the lost elder rune. What were you two thinking? A lost elder blood rune?"

"What? What do you mean us two?" I asked in surprise. "He's the one doing all the runing, not me. Hello? I'm the not-mage."

"You are his Aspis, are you not, Marked of Kali?"

Was everyone getting regular memos of my life? I had no idea how Quan would know of my new status, unless Monty shared it with her.

"Does Aspis mean babysitter?" I asked. "Everyone keeps using that word but I don't think they know what it means."

"Yes or no?" she asked, crossing her arms. "*You* are *his* Aspis."

"Yes, but I still think everyone is using that word—"

"It means you protect him from harm. You are his shield-bearer," she said with an edge. "Even when *he* is the source of that harm. That's what it means."

"Fine, you know what it means," I said, surrendering and glancing at Monty. "Have you ever tried to convince him to do, or not do, *anything*?"

"Yes, countless times, and I failed each and every time," she said, her voice softening and becoming laced with concern. "He and his family are quite stubborn. I didn't say it would be easy." She shook her head. "He also tells me you've been runically poisoned? Let me see."

Quan waved me over. As I closed the distance, I noticed movement from the front of the yacht. I paused and looked over as the pilot's chair swiveled around to face me.

"Evening, Mr. Strong," Robert said, from the pilot's chair. "It is good to see you again."

"You too, Robert," I said. "This is one impressive vessel."

"That she is, sir," Robert replied, running his hand along the wheel. "The *Mobula* is Mr. Fairchild's personal vessel, and faster than anything on, or under the water."

"I have no doubt," I said. "Did you say under?"

He tipped his cap and looked at Monty.

"Are we off, sir?" Robert asked. "As per the plan?"

"Yes, approach from the south and dock near the hospital," Monty said. "Verity will have difficulty tracking us on the river."

"Where *exactly* are we going?" I asked as I approached Quan. "Hospital? I just left Haven. Why are we going to another hospital?"

"This location is special," Monty said. "Also, Quan needs the freedom to deal with your condition, and she is here"—he gave her a sidelong glance—"unofficially."

"You're not here officially?" I asked. "What does that

mean? Is the White Phoenix going to think we kidnapped you?"

"No. Even though I'm not here as a mage of the White Phoenix, my sect leader knows where I am and my purpose here," Quan replied, as the yacht glided away from the marina. "Now, stand still and let me see how severe this poisoning is."

"Are you certain you wouldn't prefer to diagnose him when we arrive?" Monty asked. "The poisoning seems to be counteracted by his curse."

"Thank you for your expert diagnosis," she said. "If I need a second opinion, I'll make certain to consult with you. Perhaps you should check with Robert about our course to the island?"

I smiled as she gave him a look that made him decide to have an immediate conversation with Robert about where we were going.

"What island would that be?" I asked, watching Monty head to the front of the yacht. "Are we headed somewhere warm? Because that would be absolutely excellent."

"Weren't you just in Hades?" she asked. "I hear it's plenty warm there. Lakes of lava and such."

"There's warm and then there's inferno," I said, shaking my head. "Hades is not the kind of warm I enjoy."

"We're heading to Ellis Island."

"Ellis Island?" I said as images flooded my memory—unpleasant images of fighting for my and Michiko's life. "Why?"

"I understand you may have some reservations about our destination, but it can't be helped," she said, staring at me. "We need to evade discovery, and your combined signatures make that nearly impossible. Now sit still."

Ellis Island.

The last time I was on Ellis Island, Michiko was being

held captive by the Blood Hunters. I seemed to remember that the island was unfriendly to mages.

Even my curse would have problems working on Ellis Island. That was a real concern, considering I was currently poisoned and the only thing keeping me alive was my curse.

"Is Ellis Island a good idea?" I asked quickly as she placed a hand on my chest and closed her eyes. "I thought the defenses of the island made it impossible to cast."

"They are formidable," she said, keeping her eyes closed. "It will be near impossible to cast anything while on the island."

"What about my condition?" I asked. "The defenses affect my curse—you know, the curse that's keeping me alive by fighting the runic poison?"

"That does sound like a dilemma," she said with a small nod as the designs on her head and face began to glow. "You would be defenseless if Kali's curse stopped working right now. Death would follow in minutes—true death."

"Is this your way of convincing me that this is a good idea?" I said, giving her a look she couldn't see. "Because this sounds like a horribly lethal idea."

"What do you know of Ellis Island?" she asked, as she placed one hand on the other side of my chest and another on my forehead. "What have you been told?"

I tried to remember Erik's words describing the island.

"Ellis Island—the entire island—is configured with runes," I said. "It was a mage detention site, and when they decommissioned it, the Council just shuttered the entire island. No mage is crazy enough to set foot on that island."

"Exactly," she said. "For our purposes, it's perfect."

SIX

At this point I was beginning to wonder what zone I had stepped into and why Rod Serling wasn't informing me of the signpost up ahead: where I had departed my reality and entered this one, where stepping onto an island designed to kill me was the accepted plan.

"I'm not seeing how any of this is perfect," I said, once she removed her hands. "Can you clarify it for me please? Before we get on the island and I start the dying?"

"How familiar are you with ley-lines and places of power?" she asked.

"Actually, I've run into them a few times," I said. "St. Paul's in London and recently near Italy on this tiny island you would never find on a map."

"Scola Tower," she said. "I heard."

"Hold on," I said, raising a hand. "Is there some kind of Simon Information Network I'm not aware of? How is it that people know what's going on in my life without me telling them?"

She had removed her hands by this point, interlacing her

fingers as she gazed at me. It was unnerving, watching her serene expression as we discussed stepping on a deadly island.

"Are you feeling watched?" she asked with a slight smile. "Are you having feelings of persecution? Do you believe someone is after you?"

"I'm not paranoid," I said defensively. "It's happened a few times already and I know *I* never told *you* about Scola Tower."

"It's not paranoia if it's true," she said with a short nod. "You *are* being watched."

"Excuse me?" I said, not really surprised. "Watched how exactly?"

"What did you expect?" she asked. "To live a carefree life in anonymity?"

"I'm not naive," I said. "I don't expect to be anonymous when I'm walking around with the one-man wrecking mage. I just didn't expect this much attention."

"Some of this attention is misdirected, I'll grant you that much," she agreed. "Some of it, however, is your own doing. You chose to intervene between Shiva and Kali, resulting in your curse."

"There were children involved. I didn't realize—"

"You also chose not to take the shot," she said, cutting me off. "which resulted in your past coming back to pay you a visit in the form of Douglas and his associates. A situation which is still unresolved, I might add."

"No one knows about that," I said. "How *much* do you know exactly?"

"Enough to know that others know," she said as she looked over the edge of the yacht into the dark water of the river. "More than enough, actually."

"Is everyone as well-informed as you?"

"No," she said, shaking her head. "I make it a point to know what needs to be known. The White Phoenix focuses on healing. I am what's considered an outlier in the sect."

"I see," I said. "So my days of walking the shadows are over?"

"I'd say they ended the day you partnered with Tris," she said, without looking up from the river. "You just didn't know it at the time."

"I didn't ask to be in this world of magic, gods, and creatures."

"Nevertheless, you now walk in the world of magic, of the supernatural," she said, turning to face me. "It is vast and small simultaneously."

"I'm beginning to see that. Even if I wanted to hide, my energy signature after Kali upgraded my mark—and then the stormblood—mean I can't anymore."

She nodded.

"When you do what you did at Scola Tower, in a place of power, those things have a way of getting noticed," she said. "Similarly"—she glanced at where Monty stood —"when a mage—not an Archmage—uses a forbidden and lost elder blood rune, or unleashes void vortices in a populated city, like this one, it gets attention, and not just from Verity. In both cases, it's usually the wrong kind of attention."

I remembered Durga/Kali's words: *You were not the only one who noticed. Your display of power gained the attention of many.*

"Kali said as much," I said. "How much longer can we stay under the radar?"

"Stay under the radar?" she answered with a small chuckle. "You want to remain *under* the radar?"

"Well, as much as possible, yes."

"Have you not heard a word I just said?"

"I have," I said. "I just wondered if it was possible to stay off the supernatural radar for a while longer."

"Let me put it to you this way: you and Tris have taken the radar and blasted it into the heavens for all to see. There is no hiding for either of you. You and your goddess have seen to that, O Marked One."

"This attention we have attracted—?"

"You have more pressing matters to concern yourself with at the moment," she said, looking at Monty, who was approaching. "The runic poisoning is extensive, beyond my current skills to undo without risking severe damage. I can provide some relief, remove some of the damage, but this level of poisoning is like nothing I've ever seen. You need an accomplished, proficient Crimson Phoenix mage to deal with this extent of the runic damage. You need Mage Edith Alnwick—my old teacher."

"I thought you were estranged?" Monty asked. "Didn't she try to erase you?"

"We are and she did," Quan said, looking out over the river again. "She never forgave me for leaving the teachings of the Crimson Phoenix and following the White."

"Why are we calling this person again?" I asked. "She doesn't sound friendly."

"She isn't," Quan replied. "She's also the best when it comes to poisons, especially the runic sort. That being said, she may still be upset with me."

"How upset?" I asked. "Upset enough to try to end you?"

"Possibly," Quan said. "She never did take rejection well."

"She was upset you chose not to be her assassin," Monty clarified. "Does she realize that was one of the reasons the Crimson was hunted near the point of extinction?"

"Of course."

"How much of a Crimson Phoenix mage are you?"

"I am versed in the tenets of the Crimson Phoenix," she said. "The same way a doctor knows of poisons to treat them. That knowledge base differs from that of an assassin who uses poison as a weapon. More so when it comes to energy.

That is mainly the domain of the Crimson Phoenix; I am more White Phoenix than Crimson presently."

"How is your old teacher still alive?" I asked. "I thought the Crimson Phoenix were all killed?"

"It's notoriously difficult to eliminate blood mages," she said with a small shake of her head. "Edith Alnwick is a master venomancer. Killing her would be quite the feat. Many have tried, but all have died in the attempt."

"Then why did Hades mention you when I brought up the Crimson Phoenix instead of this Mage Alnwick?"

"What *exactly* did he say?"

"He said you could be of assistance," I said. "I thought he meant you could remove the poison."

"Did he say I could or would?"

I thought back to Hades' words: *You've been poisoned. Quan, however, may be of assistance.*

"He only said you could be of assistance," I said. "I should have asked what he meant by that." I shook my head. "Gods and their word games. Does this mean you can't remove it?"

"I've learned that when dealing with beings of power, it's best to be as specific as possible," she said. "They have a tendency to speak in half-truths."

"I think the word you're looking for is *lies*."

"In this case, Hades was partially correct," she said, gazing at me again. "I can be of assistance, I know the blood lessons, but I have never had to deal with a case this extensive."

"So you can't cure this poison?"

"No. No one can. The only person that can do that is the person who put it there in the first place," she said, staring at me. "Who poisoned you?"

Her question made me realize that it was very possible I had shortened my lifespan from immortal to soon to be deceased.

"I did," I said. "I was the one who poisoned myself."

She nodded.

"Then *that* is who must remove the poison," she said, pointing at me. "That is why you need Mage Alnwick. She is the one who can show you how to do that. She is the best mage to give you the proper instruction."

"What if she can't or won't?"

Quan's expression darkened.

"Then...I will attempt it," she said. "The outcome may be less than desirable. Knowing the blood lessons is not the same as transmitting them effectively. Let's hope it doesn't come to that."

"What is the cost?" I asked. "There is always a cost."

She cocked her head to one side and nodded approvingly.

"Good, you are learning," she said. "Yes, there is *always* a cost. Edith is...eccentric. I don't know what her price will be to help you, but it will be unexpected and difficult."

"Of course, because why would it be easy?"

"It rarely, if ever, is easy in situations like this," Quan replied, her voice somber. "She will want something of great value."

"I don't carry things of value."

"Not material wealth," Quan said, looking off into the distance. "She will require something of true value to you."

"I don't understand," I said, not seeing what she meant. "The only things I have of true value, besides my life, are those closest to me. What is she going to do? Ask for Peaches?"

"I don't know. She's unpredictable and adheres to rules only she understands," she said. "Prepare for any type of request."

"And if her price is too steep?"

"Refuse," Quan said. "If you are unwilling to pay the cost, say so. Do not attempt to negotiate with her. You will lose."

"Are you sure I can't just take my chances with the poison

running its course?" I asked. "This Edith sounds like bad news."

"She's not evil, per se," Quan explained. "She just has a very loose understanding about what evil is."

"That sounds like you're trying to tell me she's evil without telling me she's evil," I said. "How *loose* is her understanding?"

"Loose enough that we are finding a neutral place to summon her to us," Quan said. "A place strong enough to deter her from any rash decisions...like attempting to kill us outright."

"Is that why are we heading onto Ellis Island?"

"We aren't heading onto Ellis Island," Monty said. "The surface of the island would be a death sentence for you. If your curse ceased to function, the poison would kill you almost immediately."

I looked at Quan in confusion.

"You said we are heading to Ellis Island, but Monty says we aren't," I said. "I know I'm not at one hundred percent due to the poison, but I haven't suffered any head blows in the last twenty-four hours. What's going on?"

"I never said we were going to go *on* the island," Quan answered. "We *are* heading there, however."

"Quan is correct," Monty explained. "We *are* heading to Ellis Island; we just aren't going to step on Ellis Island."

"Then where exactly are we going? Ellis Island adjacent?"

"Close," Monty said. "We are going *under* Ellis Island."

SEVEN

"Under?" I asked, confusedly as I re-examined the yacht. "We are standing on a yacht and I'm not seeing any scuba equipment. How do you plan to go under the island? Are we teleporting the entire vessel? Can you?"

"Not without alerting Verity," Quan said. "No, this vessel is equipped to transport us."

I looked at them both as if they had lost their minds.

"Last time I checked, yachts and the vessels like them are designed to travel on the surface of the water—the *surface*."

"True," Monty said. "But this is a SuNaTran vessel. By now, you should know to expect the unexpected." He turned to Robert. "How close are we, Robert?"

"Submersion in ten minutes, sir," Robert replied without looking back. "Feel free to go below deck if you so choose."

"Submersion?" I asked. "Did he say *submersion*?"

Monty nodded.

"It's a SuNaTran vessel," Monty said simply. "That, and I think Cecil indulged in one too many conversations with Fleming."

"Fleming as in Ian Fleming? As in Bond—shaken, not stirred, James Bond?"

"Whose life was the inspiration for his famous character, yes," Monty said. "Fleming was quite fascinating. Did you know he worked for Naval Intelligence? Not a surprise, actually, that he would create a spymaster character in his stories."

"Are you saying this yacht is like some special Bond vessel?"

"Bond is a fictional character, Simon," Monty corrected. "I'm saying this vessel is some special Cecil vehicle along the lines of the Shrike we recently had the pleasure to use."

"That thing was something out of sci-fi," I said. "I'd never seen a VTOL that large, quiet, or fast."

"Indeed. Robert, please begin the submersion procedure early," Monty said. "Simon would like to see it in action." He glanced at me. "This should satisfy your curiosity."

"Right away, sir," Robert said, pressing some buttons on the console in front of him. "Please stand clear of the sides of the craft."

We moved to the center of the deck, sitting in the seats situated in pairs around a large table. The canopy that was mostly over Robert began to slide backward until it covered the entire deck, enclosing us in what I hoped was a watertight compartment.

Robert flipped a few more switches and I felt the air current from the vents around us. Robert released a lever and pushed forward on the wheel, sending the bow of the *Mobula* underwater as we dove.

I stood and moved to one side of the canopy to peer into the river as it washed over us. Peaches grumbled as we submerged, but other than that remained in place, snoring softly a few seconds later.

I noticed small wings extending from each side of the sub, making the entire vessel look like some giant—

"Ray," Monty said. "It looks like a giant manta ray."

I nodded.

"That's the first thing that came to mind," I said. "How practical is this? Ellis Island has a surface dock. What are we going to do underwater?"

"You are partially correct," Monty said. "When Ellis Island served as a mage detention facility, transportation of some of the most dangerous inmates needed to be kept a secret."

"You're telling me that Ellis Island has a submarine dock?"

"Two, actually," Monty said. "One on the north side and a matching dock on the south side of the island."

"The one near the hospital is on the south side," I said, remembering the layout of the island. "That's the one we're using?"

"Yes," Monty said, looking into the darkness of the river. "The north dock has been flooded and shut down permanently. Only the south dock near the hospital is viable."

"What about the defensive runes?" I asked, concerned that once we reached the island, my curse would stop working, making this my last yacht-sub trip ever. "Don't they work, even underwater?"

"Normally, they would," he said. "Cecil has found a workaround which allows us to use the base as long as we remain underground."

That sounded like one of Cecil's untested experiments.

"Not that I don't trust Cecil or SuNaTran," I said, "but this workaround—how many times has it been tested?"

"This will be the first time," he said, handing me a circular rune-covered pendant hanging from a silver chain. "I have every confidence in Cecil's attention to detail."

I took the pendant and stared at him for a few seconds before taking a deep breath and letting it out slowly.

"Cecil isn't a mage," I said, holding up the small pendant for inspection. "What's this supposed to do?"

"The runic buffer will create a personal neutral area around the wearer, allowing your curse to function uninterrupted by the defensive wards," he said. "As well as allowing Quan and I to cast unhindered."

"This little pendant is supposed to negate the runic defenses of Ellis Island?" I asked, still looking at the small silver pendant. It was about three inches in diameter with softly glowing, orange runes I couldn't decipher. "I'm underwhelmed and it looks cheesy."

"Be that as it may," Monty said, putting on his runic buffer. "You need to wear it or experience a horrific death by poison. Which do you prefer? Cheesiness or life?"

"I'm not a fashionista," I said, putting on the runic buffer. "Plus, I enjoy breathing. It's just that it doesn't seem powerful enough to deal with all of Ellis Island. I'm barely reading any energy from it."

"What do you mean?" Monty asked. "Why doesn't it seem powerful enough?"

"It's tiny compared to the island," I said. "I expected something enormous to negate the defenses for some time. Not some little trinket that looks like it came out of a cereal box."

"I don't understand your reference to a cereal box," he said, annoyed. "I can assure you that these were handcrafted by Cecil, a master runecrafter. They are strong enough."

"I'm just saying I would feel more comfortable if these things were industrial-sized," I said, holding the small pendant. "This thing is tiny."

"Size is irrelevant when it comes to energy manipulation," he said, slipping into professor mode. "The size of a single atom is minuscule, impossible to see with the naked eye. Yet, split a small amount, say a gram of U-235, and, well, that unleashes energy on a massively destructive scale, agreed?"

"Sure," I said. "So you're saying these will work and I won't step onto the island and drop dead a few minutes later."

"Are you having reservations?"

"Am I having reservations?" I asked, incredulously. "Am I having *reservations?*"

"I believe I just asked you that," he answered. "Are you?"

"We're in some kind of experimental super sub." I waved an arm around, "entering under an ancient mage prison designed to stop all magic once we step on the island—"

"We aren't stepping *on*—"

"Semantics, Monty," I nearly yelled, waving a hand. "This hasn't been done before and Cecil is using *us* to test out his sub and the runes at Ellis. Yes. I have reservations, plenty of them."

"I do admit a modicum of trust is required for this aspect of the mission," Monty said. "However, you *have* extended this same level of trust and more to Cecil. What is so different now?"

"I've what?" I asked. "I don't recall volunteering for some death test on Ellis Island before, or anything even close to that."

Monty stared at me for a few seconds before raising a finger as he made his point.

"Every day you revel in sitting inside a vehicle designed to kill its driver," Monty said, pointing at me. "Every day."

"I don't revel," I countered. "I appreciate."

"You sit there and accelerate the engine with that lopsided grin on your face, as the roar of that infernal engine deafens us," he said. "You revel."

"That's not reveling," I corrected. "That's *basking* in the automotive glory that is the Dark Goat Tri-Power engine. It's similar to your moaning when enjoying a good *cuppa* of Earl Grey."

"They are not the same," Monty said. "Not. Even. Close."

"True," I admitted with a small smile. "The Dark Goat beats a good cuppa of anything on any day and at any time."

Monty's lips became a thin line of disapproval as he gave me the *you have no idea what you're talking about* look.

"Regardless," he continued, "I sense no reservations from you about driving a vehicle given to us to discover the method of its destruction so that Cecil can try and destroy the Night Warden's vehicle."

"Cecil should just quit while he's behind," I said. "That beast of a car will never be destroyed. We've already seen what those runes have done to the Dark Goat, especially after that tornado of destruction."

"It did prove to be resilient."

"Resilient? The Dark Goat is indestructible," I said, realizing he was right about the risks we took. "Besides, I'm not driving it into any rivers or mage detention camps. The Dark Goat is automotive art. This boat is nice, but it's no Dark Goat. Not. Even. Close."

"I think I understand," he said with a short nod. "You're fine driving the death machine Dark Goat to your destruction as long as you look good while doing it?"

"No, you don't understand," I said. "The Dark Goat is different. It's designed—"

"To kill the driver, yes, I would say that makes it quite different," he said. "Like you said—semantics. It's the same thing. We will have to trust that Cecil knows what he's doing and wouldn't willingly send us to our deaths."

"It's the 'willingly' part that bothers me. Doesn't matter if it's unwillingly if the end result is the same. You can't blast someone to pieces and then say: 'Oops, sorry, I unwillingly shredded you to death,'" I said. "All I'm saying is that it's thin."

"Sometimes thin is all we have," he said, turning to Quan. "Do you have a way to contact Mage Alnwick when we arrive?"

Quan, who held a concerned expression on her face as she glanced at the river rushing by, nodded as we silently approached Ellis Island.

"Yes," she said, her voice barely above a whisper. "I can reach out to her, but it's her choice if she wants to respond. If she does, it will be...unpleasant."

"How bad?" I asked. "Is she going to attack us?"

"She's a Master Venomancer," Quan said as if that was enough of an answer. She continued when I gave her a blank look. "If she wanted to attack us, we would be dead before we realized we were facing an attack. She can turn the very air we breathe into a toxin."

"That sounds bad."

"It is," Quan agreed. "If she's in a good mood she may only attack me. If she's in a bad mood... You don't want to see her in a bad mood."

"We can mitigate some of the risk by using the circle in Ellis," Monty said. "It should prevent her from using her abilities on us—at least long enough for us to deal with the situation."

"I don't think the circle on Ellis is that strong," Quan warned. "It will be a minor deterrent at best."

"Maybe you should meet her on the surface of Ellis while the rest of us wait downstairs?" I said. "Won't the runes on the island neutralize her ability, too?"

"They may slow her down, but she will still retain most of her power. Did I mention she was a Master Venomancer? She predates the runes on Ellis by several centuries. They won't be an issue...for her."

"But they will be an issue for you?"

Quan nodded.

"I will be disadvantaged meeting her on the surface even with a runic buffer." She glanced at the pendant around her neck. "I wouldn't feel comfortable. I'll take my chances underground, thank you very much."

"This sounds like a horrible idea," I said. "Is there an alternative besides meeting this Poisonous Mage?"

"I highly suggest you never let her hear you refer to her as the Poisonous Mage," Quan said, her expression serious. "If you want to keep breathing, that is. She can be sensitive about how she is perceived."

"I'd be sensitive, too, if I was the equivalent of toxic magic."

Quan rubbed her face and gave me a look.

"Do not call her magic 'toxic' either," she said. "Perhaps just refrain from speaking?"

"So no other alternative?"

"Of course," Monty said. "There's always an alternative."

"Which is?"

"We let the poison in your body run its course," he said, his voice grim. "We don't know what the outcome could be. It could destroy you, or make you exponentially stronger. Most likely it will devour you internally, but we really don't know."

"Have I ever mentioned how much I enjoy mage morale moments?"

"Yes—a few times, actually."

"Hades said the same thing," I said. "Something about the outcome being interesting."

"He wasn't wrong," Quan said. "It will be interesting to see how you fare once the poison reaches your brain. There is a good chance it can make you stronger, as Tris said. However, runic poisoning can have unexpected side-effects."

I looked down at my forearms, crisscrossed with a lattice of energy.

"How much stronger can it make me?" I asked. "Strong enough to deal with major threats?"

"Strong enough to realize what is happening to you, right before your brain explodes," Quan said softly. "The current level of poisoning in your body defies explanation. You should be dead right now."

"That is not a good alternative."

"Agreed. It's time to decide to take that risk or face Mage Alnwick. Either option is risky," she said. "With Alnwick, at least you have a chance of addressing your condition and surviving mostly intact."

"Mostly intact?"

"Runic poisoning is an unknown field of study. Even among the White Phoenix, we don't see many cases of it, and none as extreme as yours," Quan said, her voice low. "Mostly intact is the most we can hope for with such a severe case."

"That's really encouraging," I said with a glare at Quan. "Those are my choices? Let it run its course and risk brain implosion or deal with the Poison—er, Venomancer, and hope for mostly intact?"

"On the bright side," Monty said, "we have established that your brain is only mostly intact. This will just bring the rest of you into alignment."

"Your humor always manages to disappoint," I said, shooting him a glare. "We go with scary option one: Angry Master Venomancer. Let's see if we survive mostly intact."

Quan nodded as we approached Ellis Island.

EIGHT

We arrived at Ellis Island in silence.

The *Mobula* banked and traveled through the river effortlessly as Robert brought her into the submarine dock below the south side of Ellis Island.

I took a moment to recall the surface layout of the island from my last visit. The island was U-shaped and turned on its side. Buildings occupied both ends of the U.

The north side held the Immigration Museum. Several other buildings were connected to this main structure. The south side held the Ellis Island Hospital Morgue—a sprawling complex of small buildings.

In the center of the U sat a large, squat building with a dock leading right into the water. It connected both ends of the island. Behind this building there was the Ellis Island Bridge leading away from the island and into New Jersey.

I thought about the last time I had used that bridge. The original Goat had been mercilessly melted by Monty's fan club right before we had escaped to London.

Now that we were going to be under the island, I figured the surface configuration wouldn't be much of an issue.

The *Mobula* surfaced and sat near one of the platforms in the dock.

"Does Verity know where we are?" I asked as we exited the *Mobula*. "Were they able to track us?"

"One moment," Monty said, raising a hand and turning to Robert. "Thank you, Robert. Please send Cecil my regards."

Robert tipped his hat.

"She's now keyed to your energy signatures," Robert said, looking from Monty to me as he moved to the side of the dock. "Mr. Fairchild would appreciate delivery of the vessel intact."

"He's leaving the super subyacht here?" I asked, shaking my head. "With us?"

"Unless you have another method for our egress from the island," Monty said, still looking at Robert, "we will do everything in our power to deliver the *Mobula* intact."

"How is he getting back?" I wondered aloud as I scanned the dock. "Is there another vessel around here?"

"Watch," Monty said, stepping back. "SuNaTran has some of the most powerful retrieval runes I have ever seen. They will work almost anywhere."

Robert removed a small fob and pressed the button. A blue-white light enveloped him, hiding him from view. A few seconds later, the light dissipated and Robert was gone.

"That's a handy thing to have."

"Indeed," Monty said. "A shame Cecil has only managed to have it work for one destination—SuNaTran."

"How upset would Cecil be if we...theoretically...damaged this subyacht?" I said. "Theoretically, of course."

"Of course," Monty said. "Theoretically, Cecil would be highly put out and find a way to make us pay, both figuratively and literally."

"That doesn't sound pleasant," I said, looking around the

dim submarine dock. "Can we make sure to return it to him in one piece?"

"We will."

"Let me clarify," I said, raising a hand. "Not return *one piece* like you did with the Duezy steering wheel. I mean, return the *entire* vessel, in working order, undamaged."

"I understood what you meant," Monty said, brushing off his jacket sleeves. "I am not solely responsible for the destruction of the vehicles Cecil loans us. We will return the *Mobula* without damage."

"You know what I've realized?"

"Please, enlighten me with your sage wisdom."

"You can't spell damage without a mage," I said. "It's right there in the word. Explains so much. Can't believe I didn't see it before."

"Your profound insights are truly staggering," he said with a huff. "Any other earth-shattering nuggets of wisdom you'd like to share?"

"Not at the moment, no."

"Good. As for your earlier question, it's unlikely Verity was able to track us here."

"Unlikely doesn't sound completely certain," I said. "Unlikely sounds like there is a chance they could have followed us."

"They managed to find your signature at Haven," Monty said, tapping his chin. "The river should have scrambled our signatures enough to provide some cover. However, they are resourceful, and they do want us dead."

"They want *you* dead," I said, wiggling my fingers. "You. Discoverer of the lost elder blood rune. They're not after me."

He raised an eyebrow.

"Really?" he answered. "I didn't notice any ogres after *me* at Haven."

"They only sent those ogres after me to get to you," I complained. "Knowing you has become hazardous to my health."

"Says the Marked of Kali, who has successors chasing us across oceans," he snapped. "You are a veritable island of safety."

I gave him a glare and could've sworn Quan stifled a laugh behind a few coughs. Peaches bumped into my leg, nearly shoving me into the water as he stepped onto the dock. I was about to explain how his nudges were getting dangerous when Quan crouched down and rubbed him on the head.

"He is such a good boy," Quan said. "Has he attained his battle form yet?"

"Battle form?" I asked. "You mean Peaches XL?"

"Peaches XL?" Quan asked. "What's that?"

"He gets ginormous and sounds like a university professor when we communicate," I said, glancing at my hellhound. "Peaches XL."

"I've never heard of it," she said. "When hellhounds mature, they have a specific battle form. He must still be too young."

"What exactly does this battle form look like?"

"It differs with each hellhound," she said. "There's a reason they are so rare. Most don't survive the transition, or they are hunted and killed before they can achieve their battle form."

"Are you saying Peaches XL is not his battle form?"

"Increasing in size and intellect is not a battle form," Quan said with a small smile. "I would argue his intellect remains the same no matter his size. His expression of that intellect may vary, but that says more about his bondmate than him."

"Basically, I'm not smart enough to understand him at his normal level, so he dumbs it down for me?"

She nodded.

"Nothing to do with your intelligence or lack thereof," she said, still rubbing his head. "You haven't advanced far enough in your power level to understand him properly. That will take at least a few decades before he can really speak to you."

"So you're saying he's really a genius hellhound?"

"His intellect is vastly superior to ours," Quan said, standing. "It's why unbonded hellhounds are so dangerous. I'm surprised you don't know this. You really should ask Hades about your hellhound's battle form."

"He didn't come with a manual, just a bottomless pit for a stomach," I said. "Besides, Hades is more the 'surprise me with the battle form' type of personality. Even if I ask, I doubt he'll share, not wanting to spoil my experience or sudden heart attack."

<She said I'm vastly superior. This is true.>

<So far, only your appetite is vastly superior to any creature I have ever seen.>

<My appetite is vastly superior because I am the most superior hellhound you know.>

<You're the only hellhound I know.>

<Which means I'm correct. See? Vastly superior. Can the angry man make some meat? Vastly superior hellhounds should have plenty of meat, superior amounts of meat.>

<I'll ask him in a bit. Hold your superior black hole of a stomach in check for a few moments.>

Peaches rumbled by my side and nudged me again. I was ready for it this time, locking my legs and standing firm. It felt like he dislocated a hip when he connected. I made a mental note to put a stop to his battering-ram nudges as I limped after Monty.

"This way," Monty said as he led us away from the dock. "We can find a suitable spot for our meeting with Mage Alnwick."

"Did you know?" I asked as we headed down the brightly lit featureless corridors of concrete. It felt like I was walking through an old abandoned war bunker where the design choice was brown concrete with a dash of mold. "About Haven?"

"You're going to have to be a bit more specific," Monty said. "What about Haven?"

"About me and Haven," I repeated. "They were using me as bait."

"You were never bait," Monty said. "They were coming for *you*. You weren't bait, you were the target."

"How did *I* become the target? You're the one that used the lost elder blood rune."

Quan coughed politely and raised a hand.

"I think I can shed some light on that," she said. "May I?"

"Please do," I said, keeping my anger in check. "Tell me why I have the mage police after me, a non-mage."

"Of course," she said as we kept walking through the maze of corridors. "It would seem to make more sense if Verity targeted Tris for his use of the elder rune. Yes?"

"That's what I was thinking, yes," I said. "I don't figure how I'm even on their radar. This is guilt by association."

"Not entirely," Quan said. "Yes, there is some of that, but Verity is in the business of upholding the tenets established long ago—especially the potential for wholesale chaos in an ordered world."

My neck tingled at her use of the old god's names.

"Not following," I said after a pause while rubbing the back of my neck. "They come across as zealots willing to accept collateral damage in their pursuit of Monty and me. They are willing to risk innocent lives to get us. Cain was a maniac in London. He didn't care what he destroyed or who was in the way if he managed to kill us."

Quan nodded.

"Verity Blades are renowned for their single-mindedness of purpose," she said. "They act with impunity when it comes to enforcement, hence their attitude regarding collateral damage."

"They act insane," I said, darkly. "Nana should have ended Cain when she had the chance."

"Not our call to make," Monty said. "Would you like to be the one to inform her how she should deal with an adversary? I doubt even my uncle Dex is *that* reckless."

"No thanks. Pass," I said with a shudder. "She seems nice and all, but the power she has and wields...it's like standing too close to the sun. I think I'd rather take a chance pissing off Josephine than facing Nana. Any day."

"That is an apt description," Monty said. "Nana gives even Dex pause, and he rarely pauses to consider anything—or anyone outside the Morrigan—a threat."

"You have to understand their mindset if you are to have a chance of confronting them," Quan said. "You have to learn how they think."

"They think any mage who uses one of their forbidden runes is a threat to the world at large," I said. "That threat needs to be eliminated at all cost. Pretty narrow-minded if you ask me."

"You missed the part of potential chaos," she said, shaking her head. "They are trained to detect patterns. A void vortex here"—she glanced at Monty—"destruction of some buildings there, and a pattern begins to emerge."

"What pattern?"

"You tell me," she said, lowering her voice. "Ever since you two joined forces, what is the common theme?"

"Saving lives and this city," I said, my voice hard. "When everyone runs away, we're the ones running toward. We run into the danger."

"Yes, this is true," she said. "However, there is more, something deeper. You know the answer."

I did. I just didn't want to say it out loud.

"Chaos," Monty said from ahead of us. "We confront chaos on a constant basis."

I knew it was true the moment he said it.

"If we don't do it, who will?" I snapped. "Like I said, we're the ones running into the fire when everyone is running away."

"This is all true. Now, see it from Verity's perspective," Quan said. "How would they view it? From the outside looking in."

I paused for a few moments and gave it thought. A chill ran down my spine as I saw what she meant.

"They would assume that we are the *cause* of the chaos," I said. "That our continued existence will ultimately bring the destruction of...everything?"

"How?" she asked gently, as we rounded another corner. "How would it happen?"

"At some point, either Monty is going to cast some ultra-nasty spell of ultimate disintegration that can't be reversed, or Peaches and I are going to go on a rampage."

"For the record, no such spell or cast exists," Monty said. "There are checks and balances against such things."

"Oh, I don't know," Quan said. "A void vortex comes close when it's cast inside a city—and you unleashed not one, but two."

"There were mitigating factors involved," Monty said. "It's a matter of nuance."

"Ah, nuance," Quan replied with a nod. "I'm sure Verity has a complete understanding of your nuanced use of forbidden runes and casts. It must be why they're responding in such a controlled and nuanced manner. This must be an overreaction on their part."

"I agree," Monty said. "But I do concede your point."

"What is the other possibility, Simon?" she asked, looking at me. "Why is Verity overreacting, according to Tris?"

"Monty, Peaches, and I are going to go nuclear and take out this entire plane somehow, while fighting a major threat," I said, hardly believing my words. "Which is insane any way you look at it. We may be powerful, but we aren't plane-ending powerful."

"Is it really insane to consider that possibility?"

"What are you trying to say?"

"Verity assesses patterns," Quan said as we reached the end of a corridor and faced a massive steel door. Monty began tracing runes and placing his hands on certain parts of the door in a pre-determined sequence. "It would seem that their assessments consider you three to be a potential threat capable of destroying this plane. Perhaps not now at your current power levels, but the potential is there—in the future."

I chuckled and then stopped when I saw her expression.

"You're serious?"

"It's not entirely far-fetched," Monty said as the door hissed open, the musty air reaching my nose. "We do pose a significant threat."

"A threat to whom?" I asked. "The last time I checked, we posed a threat only to those people and beings that wanted to wipe us, or this city, off the map."

"We *have* faced beings of considerable power and survived," Monty said. "You've been upgraded to Marked, and I recently used an elder rune. In their eyes, we are becoming stronger, which means we have become a greater threat."

"A threat that needs to be checked," Quan added, "before it's too late."

"Why does 'checked' sound like 'eliminated' in this

context?" I asked. "We would never destroy this city or the plane. I like this plane and my city. It's my home."

"Verity will not simply accept our word that we won't destroy the plane," Monty said, pulling open the door further. "Organizations like that require certainty. They deal in absolutes, not abstracts."

"Meaning they absolutely want us removed from the picture if possible," I said, "without even trying to speak to us or find a reason."

"That is not how they operate," Quan said. "They believe they hold the moral high ground. The needs of the many outweigh the needs of the few, or the one."

"Not when I'm the one."

"Agreed," Quan said. "That's my theory, at least. Perhaps, once your poisoned condition is sorted, you can have a discussion with whomever is leading the Verity Blades currently and explain it to them?"

"Tana doesn't sound like the listening type," I grumbled. "She sounds worse than Cain."

"What did you say?" Quan asked as her expression darkened. "Who did you say was leading the Blades?"

"Tana?"

"How do you know that name?" she asked, her face drawn tight. "Who gave you this information?"

"Nan, the Valkyrie watching me at Haven, shared," I said. "She described Tana as the nasty second-in-command of the Blades."

"The Bloody Dagger," Quan said in an almost whisper. "This is bad. We need to find a way to get you off-plane."

"What happened to sorting out my poison situation?" I asked, feeling the fear come off Quan in waves. "Wouldn't it be better to deal with that first?"

"You don't understand," Quan said, stepping into the room ahead of us. "Tana makes Cain look reasonable. She is certifiable and relentless. She's nearly as strong as Cain, while being highly intelligent, sadistic, and ruthless. She will enjoy torturing you before ending your lives."

"Never let it be said I don't know how to make enemies."

"This is not a joke, Simon," Quan said, angry. "If she is after you—"

"I'm not running and dying tired," I said, firmly. "If she wants to try and end me and mine, she's going to need to take a number. Now, let's get this Mage Alnwick here to deal with this poison."

I entered the room and moved to one side with Quan just staring at me before she turned to Monty.

"He's mad," she said. "Does he not appreciate the danger he's in? The danger you're all in?"

"He does," Monty said, glancing my way. "We've faced worse."

"Not worse than Tana," Quan said. "Even Verity fears her. Only Cain controlled her, and now...now he's been rendered powerless. She has free rein to do as she pleases."

"We will face her when the time comes," Monty said. "He's right, though: running is not the solution. Dealing with his condition is the immediate concern."

Quan paused for a few seconds before nodding.

"You're right of course. Apologies," she said. "I let my emotions get the best of me. Let's get this sorted."

The room beyond the door was a large meeting space, from the look of it. Several tables with chairs were spread out around the floor, and in the center of the room, I saw a large teleportation circle.

The entire room felt inviting enough, but I noticed the thickness of the door and realized the room could easily be converted into a cell with that door closed.

"What is this place?" I asked, looking around. "What's with the circle and the massive bank-vault door?"

"This is called a waystation," Monty said, stepping over to the circle. "It was used by mages long ago to reach Ellis Island and bypass the defensive runes above."

"This waystation looks like a cell," I said, still examining the large teleportation circle. "Now, why are we here?"

"That is quite the existential question," Monty said with a hint of a smile. "Why indeed?"

"Here, as in Ellis Island," I clarified. "Your drollness needs work."

Monty removed some lint from his sleeve before focusing on the circle in front of him. He crouched down and began touching parts of the outer edge of the circle.

Slowly, the circle blazed to life. Golden energy raced around the outer edge, working its way to the center and illuminating the room in a hazy golden glow.

"We need to formulate a plan against Verity, but first we need to deal with your poisoned condition," he said. "For that, we need privacy and a safe place to summon a potentially hostile Master Venomancer. This location fits both conditions."

"*If* she answers my summons," Quan said. "There is a good chance she won't. Or if she does, it will be hostile."

"Which is why Simon and I will be waiting outside while you summon your old teacher," Monty said. "If things go pear-shaped, we lock the circle and the door. She will only have one option: to leave the way she came."

"You're locking her inside with her teacher?"

"Yes," Quan said, her words firm. "If things go badly, I can deal with her."

"You said she can turn the air you breathe into poison," I reminded her. "How exactly do you 'deal' with that?"

"You remove the threat before it has a chance to attack," Quan said. "It's the same strategy Verity is trying to use with you three."

Monty nodded.

"Do you need assistance with the circle?"

"Yes, please," Quan said, looking down at the glowing circle. "It has been ages since I've used a locked circle. Can you handle the unlocking sequence while I reach out to her?"

"Yes," Monty said. "We do have options. I can always lock the circle to prevent her from entering here."

"You can try," Quan said. "It would be safer and easier to lock me in the circle with her."

"Let's hope it doesn't come to that," Monty said, glancing at Quan before he focused on the circle. "I'm ready."

"Let's begin," Quan said, kneeling and placing her hands in the center of the circle. "Ready."

NINE

Monty, with one hand on the edge of the circle, began to gesture. Violet symbols floated from his fingers into the circle. The golden glow transformed to a deep red as the energy pulsed.

I stood close to the door with Peaches by my side. My hand rested on Grim Whisper's holster. I had no illusion that if Quan was right, this Mage Alnwick could deal with anything I threw at her. Still, my palm resting on Grim Whisper gave me some sense of security, even if it was only in my mind.

Quan looked up from where she knelt, giving Monty some unspoken instruction as she shifted her hands. The energy in the circle shifted from red to blinding white, forcing me to cover my eyes.

Quan stood and stepped back out of the circle.

"Now, we wait," Quan said, her voice tense. "If the circle goes black"—she looked at me—"run and don't look back."

"What does that mean? The circle going black?"

"It means she's coming with hostile intent," Quan answered softly, her gaze locked on the circle. "This is a special circle unlike any other kind of teleportation circle. That's why it was used in a place like this."

"You could read whoever was arriving before they got here," I said, looking at the white circle. "Then prepare a defense or response."

She nodded and glanced at Monty.

"Tris, make sure it remains locked, even after her arrival."

Monty shifted his hand on the circle, shooting a violet thread of energy around the outer edge, then nodded.

The circle remained mostly white as a figure appeared in the center. Quan let out a long breath and nodded to Monty, who shifted his hand, returning the energy to a golden color.

In the center of the circle stood a tall, regal-looking woman. Her black hair was loose, falling around her shoulders. She wore a gray robe similar in style to Quan, with a black sash around her waist.

A blood-red phoenix adorned one side of her robe, similar to the white one on Quan's robe.

Her pale skin shone with an inner energy and the expression she wore was one of mild amusement. The small smile across her lips never reached her silver eyes.

Silver eyes which scanned the room and settled on Quan.

"Well met, Mage Alnwick," Quan said, giving her a slight bow. "Thank you for coming, Edith."

"Don't thank me just yet," Mage Alnwick said, her voice soft and wispy. "I may still decide to end all of you."

My grip tightened around Grim Whisper as Peaches gave off a low rumble. She didn't seem like much of a threat, but her energy signature was off the charts. The four of us combined would probably last five seconds against her—she felt that strong.

I really hoped this wasn't the last bad idea we had tried.

"Well met," Monty said, giving her a slight bow, before glancing at me to do the same.

"Well met," I said, giving her a bow. "Welcome."

"Manners," Alnwick said with a raised eyebrow. "A refreshing change, for once."

She remained in the center of the circle, glancing down at the outer violet edge with a raised eyebrow. She must've sensed that she was in a locked circle since she made no move to step out of it. She only stood absolutely still, staring at Quan.

"You summoned me," Edith continued, focused only on Quan. "Why did you call me?"

"Thank you for coming, Edith," Quan said again, repeating the short bow. "We have a situation."

"*You* have a situation," Edith said, gazing down at the circle. "I have...questions."

"Please ask," Quan said. "I will provide the answers you need."

"Doubtful," Edith said and turned to me. "Who are you?"

Well, at least she didn't arrive with a laundry list of everything I had done in the last few months. It was actually surprising and took me off-guard for a few seconds.

"Does he understand English?" Edith continued as she glanced at Quan. "Is he mute?"

"He does," Quan replied, giving me a look. "He's just a little surprised at meeting you."

"I should say so," Edith said, narrowing her eyes at me. "I'm surprised he's still living with that much poison in his body." She focused on me again. "Who are you? More importantly, how are you still alive?"

"I'm sorry," I said, the words tumbling out. "My name is Simon Strong and I'm poisoned."

It sounded like I had stepped into some kind of self-help meeting. She crossed her arms and nodded at me.

"I noticed," she said. "How? Which enemy hates you to

such a degree that they would unleash this much poison on you?"

"None," I said. "I mean—"

"You have no enemies?" she said, incredulously. "I find that difficult to believe. If my apprentice is contacting me after so long, she must be desperate. If she is willing to reach out to me, it means you are facing some formidable enemies or are monumentally suicidal. Which is it?"

"Formidable enemies," I said. "But they didn't poison me."

"Then who?"

"I poisoned myself," I said, and explained how it happened without going into too much detail. "I didn't think—"

"There, I agree," Edith said, cutting me off with a raised finger. "Trying to divert a ley-line at your current level of power is a death sentence. Who is after you?"

I saw no sense in lying. She would either help or she wouldn't.

"Verity," I said. "Have you heard—?"

"Verity? Impressive," she said, examining me again. "Surely they aren't after only you." She gave Monty a sidelong glance. "What could you possibly have done to garner their attention? I mean aside from trying to end your life by diverting an active ley-line. Your power level is negligible at best. Why would they be interested in apprehending *you*?"

I explained Quan's recent theories about why Verity would be after me. Even though the group wasn't common knowledge, it seemed enough people knew of their existence to make me pause. I noticed that the mages who did know of Verity were of the powerful, avoid-whenever-possible' kind.

"That sounds like my apprentice," Edith said, glancing at Quan. "Am I correct?"

Quan nodded.

"Am I also to assume you are responsible for keeping this

circle locked?" Edith asked, narrowing her eyes at Quan. "This was your idea?"

"Yes," Quan said, with a hint of defiance. "You have been known to be unreasonable in the past, with lethal results. I thought it prudent to maintain it locked while we spoke."

"A wise choice," Edith said with a nod as she assessed the circle she stood in. "Futile but wise. Do you believe this theory you espouse?"

"It makes the most sense," Quan said. "They pose a threat that needs to be eliminated. Verity has always acted proactively when it comes to potential threats, and with Cain incapacitated—"

"This is why I accepted your refusal to follow my path," Edith said after a few moments. "You were always gifted at seeing the trees, completely missing the forest."

"You what?" Quan asked, seemingly momentarily thrown off. "You accepted? I left of my own accord."

"Of course you did," Edith said with a thin smile. "Which is why I accepted."

It was the kind of smile that made you realize you were still getting up to speed when someone had finished the race ages ago. Quan was still searching for words when Monty stepped forward.

"Tristan Montague," he said, placing a hand against his chest and bowing slightly. "You honor us with your presence."

"Montague?" Edith said, raising an eyebrow. "Related to Dexter?"

"My uncle," Monty said. "On my father's side."

"It certainly wouldn't be on your mother's," Edith said, giving Monty the once over. "She was... I'm so sorry for your loss. I heard about Connor."

"Thank you," Monty said. "You knew my mother?"

"And your father, as well as the black sheep of the family

that is Dexter Montague," she said with a small smile. "Is he still getting up to mischief?"

"You could say that," Monty said, but his voice was guarded. "They never mentioned you."

"Do you know every one of uncle's associates?" she asked. "I daresay you don't. He moved in less than savory circles, if memory serves."

"That he did," Monty said, stepping back. "Thank you for coming."

"Well, that explains much of this," Edith said. "If you want to know why Verity is after you, aside from fanciful theories"—she looked at Quan—"look no further than Dexter Montague."

"What?" Monty said, surprised. "How is my uncle involved?"

"Have you asked him?" Edith asked. "What he did?"

I was completely lost, and judging from the expressions on Quan's and Monty's faces, so were they.

"What did he do?" I asked. "Why is Verity after him?"

"It's more what he didn't do," Edith said. "They aren't after him, are they? Of course, this is irrelevant to your immediate situation. You are going to die if we don't address your tainted blood. Even with that curse, it's only a matter of time —days, maybe months, but...yes." She gave me a curt nod. "You will expire...painfully."

She had my complete attention.

"I thought I could let it run its course if there was no way around it," I said. "I was told that was an option."

Edith crossed her arms and stared at me.

"A lethal one, yes," Edith said, her voice low. "If you allow this poison to... 'run its course', as you say, your end will be a gruesome agony."

"Can I reverse it?"

"The question is: do you want to?" she answered. "The

pain you will go through will make you wish you were dead several times over. Even then, there are no guarantees. This level of poisoning is rare. Surviving it rarer still."

"Do I have a choice?" I asked. "I'd prefer not dying if that's okay."

She turned to face Quan.

"Why haven't you attempted to reverse the poison?" Edith asked, still smiling, but I saw the contempt in her eyes. "I trained you to deal with something like this. Surely you haven't forgotten the blood lessons."

"I haven't," Quan said. "This...this is a runic poisoning I have never encountered. I don't think—"

"There is no need to think," Edith said, cutting her off. "You must act. You have the information and the ability. What you lack is the will to do what must be done. This is why you left me and the Crimson Phoenix. You are weak."

"A little harsh, don't you think?" I said. "Maybe she just doesn't want to risk—"

"Simon," Quan said. "She's right. I wasn't willing to do what was required to remain in the Crimson Phoenix."

Edith turned to me, narrowing her eyes again.

"You, on the other hand," she said. "Not a mage, but something else...something complex and complicated. You know what it means to do what is necessary, to make sacrifices, even if it means your life, don't you?"

I remained silent, not appreciating psychotherapy hour.

"Can you reverse the poison?" I asked again, losing my patience. I was getting the feeling that Edith enjoyed hearing her voice and chastising Quan more than offering any kind of real help. "Or are you here just to insult your former student?"

Edith smiled again and my blood ran cold. This was someone who enjoyed death, both in seeing it and causing it. She was dangerous and she reveled in that fact.

"I can reverse it, but why *should* I?" Edith said. "I fail to see a compelling reason to offer you any assistance. What can you give me?"

"What do you want?"

A dangerous question. She smiled again—a snake closing in on the scared mouse.

"There is the matter of the cost," Edith said, lowering her voice as she gestured, materializing a chair. She sat back in the chair and crossed her legs. "You may not be able to pay my price for the blood lesson."

"Blood lesson?" I asked, glancing at Quan. "Singular?"

"Yes," she said. "You will only need one if I do it, but perform it incorrectly and it's the last lesson you will ever attempt. The lesson I intend to use is named the Crimson Dream."

Quan gasped before composing herself.

"See?" Edith continued, pointing a finger at Quan. "My apprentice knows of it. In fact, I taught it to her long ago, but she was never willing to execute it, even when her friend lay dying in her arms. She preferred to use a White Phoenix cast to purge the toxins. How did that work out for you, apprentice?"

"I...I failed," Quan said, quietly. "Lyn died in my arms. My nexus purifier failed."

"No," Edith countered. "The nexus purifier is even more potent than my Crimson Dream. *It* didn't fail...you failed."

"A nexus purifier?" Monty said, surprise in his voice as he looked at Quan. "You know this cast?"

"Yes," Quan said. "It is—"

"A lost elder rune," Monty finished. "The world ender. You attempted to cast this—alone?"

"I was desperate," Quan explained. "I thought...I thought I could cast it and save Lyn. I was wrong. The cast failed. I failed."

"Because you were *weak*," Edith snarled, waving a hand in Quan's direction. "You possessed the power to save her; I *gave* you the power to save her, and *you* let her die."

"I'm...I'm sorry," Quan said, her eyes becoming bright with tears. "I tried everything."

"No! Not everything, my dear," Edith said, regaining her composure. "You didn't try the Crimson Dream I gave you, did you? You let my sweet, sweet Lyn die because you were too much of a coward."

"I didn't know," Quan said. "I didn't know the cost. I was young and scared. I didn't know. I couldn't... It was too much."

Edith's expression hardened.

"Excuses," Edith said. "All I hear are the same excuses." She turned to me, dismissing Quan. "What shall it be, Simon Strong? It's clear my apprentice is too fearful to attempt to save you, even possessing the knowledge to do so."

I looked from Monty to Quan to Peaches.

It wasn't like I had much of a choice.

If I didn't take this opportunity, it sounded like certain death, and if I did it was possibly death with a chance at living, and plenty of pain.

Something still felt off.

Why did Quan refuse to even try, calling Edith instead? Why had Hades told me he wasn't implying my death by my letting the poison run its course?

Too many unanswered questions.

The pain, was by now, a familiar part of my life. I somehow knew it would be part of this equation. A part of my brain pointed out that Durga/Kali probably knew how to reverse my condition and had chosen not to do so.

She'd probably call it a growing experience.

I really hated gods and their games.

"Why?" I asked. "Why would you help me?"

"I haven't agreed to yet," she said. "You may not want my help after I tell you the cost."

"What is the cost?" I asked, warily. "What do you want?"

"There is a rare poison with no known antidote," she said. "It's called the Dragons Breath."

Quan paled at the mention of the name.

"We can't help you," Quan said, quickly. "Simon, we will find another way."

"There is no other way," Edith said. "Look again, my apprentice, and tell me if I lie. He is running out of time, and you can't—or won't—help him."

Quan looked away and I knew Edith was telling the truth.

"The Dragons Breath is a myth," Quan said. "No one has been able to create a stable version. It's impossible."

"Improbable, not impossible," Edith corrected. "I have almost everything I need. Except one important ingredient."

"What?" I asked. "Eye of newt? Eyelashes of a fairy? Whiskers of an enchanted wombat? What is this ingredient?"

Edith laughed, but her eyes held death.

"Simon," Quan said, warning me. "Don't. Just don't."

"Blood," Edith said. "A particular type of blood."

"You knew," Quan said. "You've known all this time."

Edith gave Quan a withering glare.

"I am a Master Venomancer," Edith said. "It is my *business* to know of these things...*medic*."

Edith said the last word with disgust as she stared at Quan.

"What kind of blood?" Monty asked, warily. "You said you needed a particular type of blood?"

Edith nodded, then focused on me.

"It's nearly impossible to get this ingredient due to the risks involved," Edith said, still focused on me. "The blood I require is dragon's blood."

I breathed out a sigh of relief and chuckled.

"Sorry to hear that," I said with a smile. "No one here is a dragon."

I looked around and realized I was the only one smiling.

"This is true," Edith said, "The Marked of Kali may possess a secret no one is aware of, not even him."

"Secret? What are you talking about?"

"You've been dragonblooded," Edith said. "I need *your* blood."

"Marked of Kali?" I said. "How do you—?"

"Everyone knows about Simon Strong, the Marked of Kali," Edith said. "In fact, there are some very angry mages looking for you."

Shit. That sounds like Verity.

"I'm sorry?" I said, acting confused. "You must have me confused with someone else."

"I don't think so," Edith said. "I'm here for your blood, as per my agreement."

"I don't remember this agreement."

"I never said I made it with you," Edith answered and sniffed the air. "Your blood will do nicely, yes."

"My blood?" I asked, realizing there was much more going on than I could see. "You mean a sample?"

"No, my dear," Edith answered sweetly. "I need your blood. All of it."

TEN

"You must have me confused with some other Marked of Kali," I said, with a shake of my head. "I don't have dragonblood and I'm in no way shape or form related to dragons. Plus, I need my blood. All of it."

Who did she make an agreement with?

"Don't be dense," Edith snapped. "I never said you were a dragon. I said you've been dragonblooded. Your blood has been exposed to dragon's blood. My senses never lie. That is the cost—your blood. All of it."

I looked down at the circle keeping her contained. As long as it could keep her in place, I was safe. If she came this far, I figured it was important to know what she was trying to do.

"What does this Dragons Breath do exactly?" I asked. "How does it work?"

"The Dragons Breath is a toxin of myth," Quan started, glancing at Edith. "It's an odorless, colorless, tasteless, flammable poison. Think carbon monoxide to the tenth power of potency. It also has one specific property, that makes it a horrific weapon."

"It's no myth," Edith said. "I have managed to stabilize a working sample. Small, but promising."

What?" I asked, staring at Edith before turning to Quan. "What does this Dragons Breath do?"

"It specifically targets magic users, causing an erasure before spontaneous immolation," Quan said. "To the untrained eye, the target mage would appear to set themselves on fire. It can't be traced after the target is rendered to ash."

"Hence the name," Monty said, darkly. "No mage would be safe from an attack like that."

"True," Edith said. "There is no counter to the Dragons Breath."

I turned to Edith.

"Why would you need something like that?" I asked. "That sounds like an assassin's weapon."

"I know," Edith said matter-of-factly. "What do you think I am? A medic? I kill people. Mages especially."

I glanced at Quan.

"This was your idea of a plan?" I asked. "Asking the mage assassin for help?"

"That was long ago," Quan said. "I had hoped that by now—"

"Ever the optimist," Edith said, cutting Quan off. "This is the reason you were unfit for the Crimson Phoenix. You believe in the inherent good of people. I prefer to live in reality. People, mages...at their core, beyond the self-serving platitudes and hollow words, are evil, deserving of death."

It was clear Edith had some major unresolved anger toward mages.

"You want to kill mages?" I said, whirling on Edith. "You want me to give you my blood to help you kill mages? Are you insane?"

"Not kill," she said. "Eradicate. Remove from existence. Erase."

I stared at her for a few seconds, assessing just how far off the deep end she was. From the look she gave me, she was Mariana Trench deep.

"Oh, excuse me...not kill," I said, staring at her. "Erase and eradicate. Well, that makes it all okay then. You are a special kind of broken, aren't you?"

"Simon..." Quan said, her voice a warning. "Mage Alnwick, he didn't mean—"

Edith hissed while raising a hand.

"Don't you dare apologize to me, you mewling excuse for a mage," Edith spat, impaling Quan with a look. "He may be a dead man walking but at the very least he has a spine."

"*You* are insane," I said. "Who did you make an arrangement with?"

"Am I insane?" Edith said with a lethal smile. "No, no. I'm not insane. What I do with your blood is none of your concern. Whether or not you give it to me willingly, I *will* take it. I only need to wait until you die or are killed. I have plenty of time...do you?"

"Go the fuck back where you came from," I said. "You want me to give you my blood so you can go on a mage killing spree, creating some super toxin no one can stop?"

"Yes," she said simply. "You're not a mage. I would expect you to possess some understanding." She looked over at Monty and Quan with an expression of disgust. "Magic users wield power for their own benefit, existing on the fringes of society like parasites. They help no one. This world would be better off if mages never existed."

I stared hard at her.

"Aren't you a magic user?" I said. "Does this new world include removing yourself, too?"

"Are you saying I'm wrong?" she asked. "You've dealt with mages and their ilk. How has the experience been? Sunshine and rainbows? No. I'll tell you how it has been. See if this sounds familiar: constantly running for your life, avoiding enemies who want you dead. Currently, you are fighting for your immortal life. This poison running through your veins, why is it there? Your proximity to mages, that's why. Is this the existence you wish?"

"It wasn't because of the mages."

"Never having a moment's rest," she continued. "Constantly being used as a pawn. Did anyone ever ask you what *you* wanted? If this was the life *you* wanted? I doubt it. Mages only leave destruction in their wake. This is why they need to be removed—all of them."

I had said many of the same words in the past, back before I understood what mages and magic users did in the world. Yes, many times they created difficult situations or even made them worse, but without mages, mages like Monty who were willing to risk everything to protect this city and plane, we would be at the mercy of beings who would destroy everything...just because they could.

"You know I'm right," she almost whispered. "I can see it in your eyes. You have thought the exact same thing. This world would be better off without mages and magic."

The insanity in her eyes did a little dance and I realized there was no reasoning with her. Whether someone had fed her these beliefs, or she had created them herself, there was no shaking her from this point of view. This was the hill she was willing to die on...literally.

"You are wrong," I said, staring back at the abyss of madness that was her gaze. "These mages, these people, are my friends, my family. I chose to be here. Chose to have them in my life."

"Whatever you need to tell yourself to sleep at night," she said, waving my words away. "I know the truth. The real poison in your body is being in proximity to magic users. *They* are the real poison."

"You really are batshit psycho," I shot back. "*That* is the truth."

She dropped her gaze to the floor before slowly looking into my eyes again. A smile crossed her lips. It was in that moment that I realized just how insane she was. She never intended to help us. She was here to eliminate us. She was buying time.

She was the distraction.

"Excuse me?" Edith said, standing and letting her hands fall to her sides. I saw the depth of her psychopathy then. It was always in the eyes, sooner or later. "You think *you* can speak to *me* that way? Do you know who I am? What I am? I was killing mages before you were a thought in your father's loins."

After a few seconds of consideration, I realized I may have been a bit hasty in my reaction to her request. Too late now. In for a penny, in for a pound.

"Does it matter? I know I'd rather take my chances on my own than help you make this Dragons Breath poison," I said, stepping back away from her and the circle. "You won't be getting *any* of my blood."

"*That* is where you are mistaken, Marked One," Edith said, raising an energy-covered hand and slamming it into the floor, sending cracks through the circle, but not breaking it. Tremors shook the sub dock. "Did you really think this simple circle could hold me?"

The circle flickered, but held Edith in place. One more strike like that and she would be free. Explosions rocked the building above us as I glanced to Monty and Quan.

"We expecting any other deranged mages?"

"Verity," Monty said, looking up. "They, too, must have found a way through the defenses."

"How did they find us?"

"They didn't," Monty said, looking slowly at Edith. "*She* led them here. Her arrangement—it must be with Verity."

Edith gave Monty a mock bow with flourish.

"Astute, Montague," Edith said. "It seems they want you all very dead. I agreed to help them on the condition I get what I wanted."

"You bitch," Quan said. "You brought them here?"

"Look at *you*," Edith said with a small laugh. "Finally showing some fire. A shame it is too little, too late," Edith said, looking at me. "Give me what I want and I promise your end will be swift. I doubt Verity will make you the same offer. I hear Tana can be quite unreasonable."

More explosions.

"They are working their way down here," Quan said, looking at her old teacher. "You haven't changed. I thought after all these years you would try to make amends, become a different person."

"*I* need to make amends?" Edith growled. "*You* let my Lyn die!"

"After *you* poisoned her to test me!" Quan yelled back. "What kind of teacher poisons her own students? What kind of test is that?"

"A true one," Edith said, her voice laced with pain, anger and ample doses of crazy. "I believed in you and you failed her. You failed me."

"This was a mistake," Quan said, shaking her head. "I thought we could salvage something between us, that you would have come to your senses, but I see now: you have left reason behind. You've surrendered to your madness."

Edith laughed then—proving to me that she had definitely embraced the madness Quan was talking about. This had gone sideways in the worst possible way.

We needed to get out. Now.

"And you are still the naive child I left all those years ago," Edith said, her voice laced with hatred. "The scorpion does not apologize for being a scorpion. I will end you this time, and take what I came for." She glanced at me. "None of you will leave this place alive."

Another series of explosions, closer this time.

"We need to go," I said, heading out of the room. "Now."

Monty, Peaches, and I headed to the door. Quan remained behind.

"What are you doing?" I asked as I looked back at her. "We need to go."

"I'm right behind you," Quan said. "If I don't stop her here, she will never stop chasing you, chasing us. This is my only chance. Go."

"Do stay," Edith said. "We have so much catching up to do."

"Quan," Monty warned, "this is unwise. The explosions will compromise the integrity of the lower levels. You'll be buried alive down here. We need to—"

"Go. Now," Quan said, firmly as she faced Edith. "I *will* catch up."

The designs on Quan's face and head began to glow as the sub dock shook with tremors. More explosions rocked the lower level.

We were running out of time. Monty took a step in Quan's direction as she whirled on us and extended both hands, unleashing a blast of white energy our way.

It shoved us out of the room and slammed the door shut behind us. Cracks appeared in the door as Monty tried to get it open again and failed.

"I can't get it open," Monty said, pounding a fist in the concrete. "She's going to die in there!"

"We need to get to the sub," I said as I crouched down next to Peaches. "This place is coming down."

"Did you not hear a word I just said?" Monty said, whirling on me and pointing at the door. "She is going to *die* in there."

"I heard you loud and clear," I said. "Do you think she would want us *all* to die down here?"

He clenched his fists as he turned back to the door, letting out a deep breath.

"She's my friend," he said, his voice somber. "I don't abandon my friends."

"I know," I said, looking at the cracked door. "That door doesn't look easy. Quan wouldn't want you to throw your life away trying to open it, would she?"

"No. No, she wouldn't," he said, in resignation. "We need to get to the *Mobula*. There's no way I can form a circle down here; the defenses would prevent it. That's our only way out. On the surface of the island, I can try to key into her signature."

"Would you be able to cast?"

He looked down at the pendant around his neck.

"I think so," he said, urgency lacing his voice. "I'm not going to leave her in there."

"One second," I said, holding Peaches' massive head in my hands. "I need a moment."

The sub dock shook with tremors again as Monty just stared at me in shock.

"A moment ago you were expressing our need to exit the premises," he said, raising his voice and waving an arm around. "Now, you need a moment?"

"One moment without an angry mage yelling in my ear would be nice," I said. "Start heading back. I know the way."

"Absolutely not," he said, looking at the door. "I'm not losing anyone else tonight."

"Then I need you to be quiet," I said. "We're not leaving Quan."

<Hey, boy. Can you get the lady with no hair?>

Peaches looked at the massive door and sniffed the air.

<I can try. The door is hard.>

I didn't know exactly what that meant, but if Quan had a chance of escaping that room, it would be with Peaches' plane-walking.

<I need you to get her and bring her to the boat as fast as you can. Can you do that?>

<For extra meat?>

<For all the meat you can eat until you're full.>

<I'm never full.>

I smiled, rubbed his head before giving him a tight hug and dodging a slobbering.

"Go get her," I said before standing and turning to Monty. "Let's go."

We set off at a run as Peaches blinked out.

ELEVEN

We ran down several empty corridors.

I could tell Monty was upset at not being able to open the door. I think he was more upset at Quan for taking Edith on alone. With each tremor, the lights in the corridor flickered as the power was interrupted.

"If anyone can get her out, Peaches can," I said, as we moved quickly down the corridor. "He can do it."

Monty grunted in response and then came to a stop.

Ahead of us were two Verity agents.

They were dressed in the typical mageiform: dark suit, white shirt, and red tie. I could tell the suits they wore weren't the usual upscale runed Zegna mage wear I was used to seeing on Monty.

"We've located them," Left Suit said to no one in particular. "Collapse on my position."

"That doesn't sound good," I said under my breath. "They have working comms down here?"

"It would appear so," Monty said. "We don't have time to spare."

"Tristan Montague and Simon Strong you are hereby

ordered to surrender, by the authority of Verity and the High Tribunal," Right Suit ordered. "If you resist, we will be forced to use—"

A beam of violet energy punched Right Suit in the face, lifting him from his feet and slamming him into the wall. Left Suit, with an expression of shock, turned to look at his partner take flight past him before turning back to face Monty.

It was too late.

Several white orbs punched into Left Suit's chest and face, knocking him unconscious. Monty proceeded to continue running down the corridor.

I kept pace behind him.

I didn't see any hand gestures or finger wiggling. One moment the Verity agents were in front of us, and the next, Monty had unleashed a magical pain tango, removing them.

I didn't even sense a spooling of energy. His response was a spontaneous explosion of magical energy.

He was getting scary.

"You didn't—?" I started. "Did you?"

"Of course not," Monty said without looking back. "They didn't deserve to die. They were less than an inconvenience. I felt I dealt with them appropriately."

"I think they would disagree."

"Fortunately, their opinion on the matter is irrelevant," he said and gave me a quick glance. "You really thought me capable of a summary execution?"

"No," I said, and meant it. "Never."

"They will regain consciousness with massive headaches," he said. "That will be the extent of their pain, aside from bruised bodies."

"Those were Blades?"

"The Book," Monty said, picking up the pace. "Blades wouldn't have bothered with telling us to surrender. They would have attacked on sight. It would seem Verity sent The Book first to slow us down."

"Redshirts," I said. "The Book are the redshirts."

"They weren't wearing red shirts," Monty said. "Granted, their suits are of somewhat inferior quality to other mages, but their shirts weren't red. That would just be poor fashion sense."

I stared at him in silence for a few seconds as we kept moving.

"I'm glad you didn't disintegrate them."

"The situation didn't warrant taking their lives," he said. "We were not in mortal danger."

"I'm just making sure you haven't gone full Sith on me. You know, lost elder blood runes and the like. Don't want you going over to the dark side."

"No Montague has ever become a dark mage in the history of my family," he said. "Not even my uncle, and his choices have been... questionable at times. I'm not about to start a precedent now, despite what Verity claims."

"We really do need to have a conversation with Dex," I said as we turned another corner and headed down a short corridor to the *Mobula*. "If we can believe anything Edith said."

"Unlikely," he said. "She's either working with or for Verity and wants your blood. All of it."

"I got that," I said as my expression darkened. "She made it clear all mages need to die. Sounds familiar?"

He nodded.

"Evers."

"Well, let's add one more batshit psycho member to the ever growing Kill Simon Fan Club," I said. "I will never, ever complain that my life is boring...ever."

"You do manage to attract some fascinatingly deranged individuals," he said, as we jumped on the deck of the *Mobula*.

Monty looked around, concern etched on his face. "Where is your creature?"

"He'll get her," I said. "I promised him extra meat."

"It's unnerving to think that the fate of my friend is in the jaws of your perpetually starving hellhound, who is, at this very moment, striving to do his best because you promised him...extra meat?"

"Meat is Life," I said, "especially for a hellhound."

"You'll forgive my skepticism," Monty said. "The runes on that door were ancient and designed to prevent breaches. This was a detention facility, after all."

"Peaches is a purebred hellhound. His dad is the gate-keeper of Hades, which is older than this place, I'm guessing," I said. "I'm putting my money on my hellhound's ancient and excellent genes to get through that door."

"Not like we have much of a choice at the moment," Monty said.

"If anyone can get her out of there, it's him," I said, looking at the pilot's console. "Let's get this sub moving. Peaches can find me wherever I am. I'd rather not run into more of Verity while waiting for him. Can you pilot this thing?"

"If I have to, yes."

"You have to," I said, sensing an increasing energy signature heading our way. "Now would be good."

I saw a slim figure heading down the corridor, exuding a major energy signature. I could tell it was a female, but I couldn't see her face in the dim light of the corridor.

"I think," Monty said, stepping back onto the dock, "*you'd* better get the boat started and ready for a hasty departure."

"What are you talking about?" I hissed. "This isn't the Dark Goat."

"The controls are simple, and the *Mobula* is keyed to you

as well," Monty said without looking away from the corridor. "Get it started and ready to leave immediately."

"Who is that?"

"That would be a Blade," Monty said, shaking out his hands as the figure approached. "A dangerous one, at that."

The figure stepped onto a platform on the sub dock.

"Tristan Montague," the woman said, stepping forward. "I've been looking forward to this for a long time."

"Hello, Ines," Monty said with a slight nod. "I'm really pressed for time at the moment. Can we schedule our death match for later?"

She gave him a slow smile.

"No," she said, forming black orbs in her hands. "The High Tribunal wants you erased and dead. This isn't personal."

"Except it is, isn't it?"

"A little."

She unleashed the orbs at Monty.

TWELVE

Monty waved a hand and deflected the orbs into the water, where they exploded, sending geysers shooting up into the ceiling of the dock.

Ines raised an eyebrow in appreciation.

She was dressed in an upscale Zegna suit with flowing red runes pulsing softly across the fabric. The energy coming off of her dwarfed the energy signatures of the Verity Book agents we'd encountered earlier.

She kept her jet-black hair short and looked to be in her mid-forties, which I knew meant nothing with mages, especially if she knew Monty. Her deep, dark brown eyes were filled with malice and determination.

This mage had something to prove.

"She looks dangerous," I said. "Friend of yours?"

"Once, long ago, when we were both much younger."

"Right, I'm going to start the boat," I said. "You two catch up."

"Starting the boat is an excellent idea," Monty said as I started backing up to the pilot's chair. "We can't face her in here in a protracted fight. I'll buy us some time until your creature arrives."

Hopefully with Quan.

Ines looked like she was heading to a power meeting with some bankers as she crossed the dock.

"You should have surrendered to the Book," she said. "But I knew you wouldn't. You were always so arrogant. Why did you kill them?"

Monty kept his face impassive as he stared back at her.

"I didn't," he said as she gestured, materializing a pair of heads onto the dock: the Verity Book agents, currently missing their bodies. Both of their faces held expressions of fear and surprise. Monty gazed down at the heads for a second. "But *you* did, it would seem."

"I did," she said with a short nod. "They were incompetent and lost their heads when they encountered the murderous, rogue dark mage Tristan Montague. Your reputation precedes you."

"I didn't realize I was known as murderous," Monty said. "Rogue, I can accept—not murderous."

"I'm changing the narrative," Ines said. "You then proceeded to exterminate them without a second thought. It's still a rough theory, but the final report will be something along those lines. What do you think?"

"I think...Verity suits you," Monty said. "You always were something of a sadist."

"Thank you," she said. "Are you going to make this boring and surrender?"

"Far be it from me to deprive you of some enjoyment," he said. "Your casts will be futile in this place. The dampening effect rendered your orbs ineffective."

"I noticed," she said, glancing at the water, extending a hand and materializing a silver-black blade. "I'll have to resort to the tried and true method of mage extermination."

Monty reached behind him and formed his cry-babies—The Sorrows.

"Why are you here?" Monty asked. "I find it hard to believe the High Tribunal would dispatch you here because I used a lost elder rune."

"I'll humor you, if only to help you realize that the world doesn't revolve around the Montagues," she said, moving to a larger part of the dock. "You made an enemy of Cain. That was unwise."

"It couldn't be helped," Monty said, stepping over to where Ines was. "He *was* trying to kill us, *and* he angered Nana. I'm amazed she left him alive."

"Fair enough," she conceded. "Then there's the matter of your friend over there turning into a dark worshipper of Kali. You know where Verity stands on these things. They hold a dim view of death goddesses in particular."

"Dark worshipper?" Monty said. "Who?"

"Simon Strong," Ines said. "Currently bonded to a hellhound, and presently the Marked of Kali." She glanced my way and narrowed her eyes at me. "He is, as of this moment, channeling enough runic poison to kill everything short of an Archmage—except he isn't an Archmage—and he isn't dead, is he? How do *you* explain it?"

"He has a particularly strong constitution?" Monty said as I gave him ten points for an excellent comeback. "The poison proves nothing."

"His not being dead makes a strong case for a favor from Kali," Ines said. "It's making me think your Simon Strong is going dark. Plus, he's not dying. You'll forgive me for thinking he may be the next dark immortal. Verity will not—*cannot* —allow that."

"Supposition and conjecture," Monty replied, measuring his words carefully. "Your theory proves nothing."

"It proves *everything*," Ines snapped. "He should be dead,

but he isn't. He serves Kali, which means he serves death. *You* used a lost elder blood rune—are you mad? What were you thinking? Did you really think that would go unnoticed?"

"I had hoped it would be overlooked," Monty said. "There were extenuating circumstances. We were facing an agent of Chaos."

"Of course there were," she said. "Then there's the hellhound. The last time a mortal bonded to a hellhound, it took an entire sect to put them down in battle formation. The losses, both in lives and property, were catastrophic. We would prefer not to revisit that circumstance again —ever."

"Is that the royal *we,* or have you started referring to yourself in the plural these days?" Monty asked. "I'm curious."

"I'm Tana's second," Ines said, her voice laced with death. "Third-in-command in the Blades. I speak for Verity in her absence."

"Royal we it is, then," he said. "Congratulations on your advancement. Your father would be absolutely repulsed."

"Don't you dare mention my father," she hissed. "You have no right."

"Don't I?"

"*We* will not face another mortal bonded to a hellhound," she stated, ignoring his reply, "much less a potential dark immortal."

"Understandably so," Monty said, his voice hard. "You would lose this time. Are these all of your accusations? They seem a little thin."

"There's one more thing," Ines said, stepping into a defensive stance. "The old god is stirring."

"There are so many," Monty said, staring at Ines. "It's hard to keep track. Can you elaborate on which old god?"

"Chaos," Ines said, the word a dagger. "His agents—as you call them—are showing heightened levels of activity. Imagine our surprise when we discovered all of this activity, all of this *chaos*, was mostly directed at you two."

"We have been popular as of late," Monty said. "So far everything you said proves nothing."

"You deny it?"

"Let me humor *you*, since you seem to be misinformed."

"Please."

"Simon garnered the attention of Kali, by interfering in a five-thousand-year-old plan she had devised," he said, causing me to wince at the memory. "I daresay anyone—especially a goddess of Kali's reputation—would be slightly put out at his interference. She extracted her own form of justice, and in his defense, he saved children. I'm certain if you asked him, he would do it again without hesitation."

"How noble," Ines scoffed. "And the hellhound?"

"A gift from a friend," Monty said. "Peculiar, perhaps. Eccentric, certainly, but not unprecedented."

"A friend? What kind of friend gifts *hellhounds*?"

"Hades."

"Hades?" Ines asked, surprise lacing her voice. "*The* Hades?"

"Unless you know of another?"

"That doesn't explain the chaos around you two."

"Chaos is chaos," Monty said in his best magespeak. "I would hazard to say that our confronting and thwarting his plans makes us agents of Order. Wouldn't you agree?"

Ines remained silent.

"Why not admit that this has everything to do with my uncle, and all of this is some kind of smokescreen?" Monty continued. "Or are you not allowed to discuss the real motive behind your attack here? Did the Tribunal sanction the use of an assassin venomancer, or was that all Cain?"

Ines' expression darkened.

"Mage Alnwick was cleared by Cain," she said. "She was

able to aid in locating Strong due to the concentration of poison in his system."

"Of course," he said. "Now here you are, because you, and especially the Tribunal know that facing off against my uncle directly would be a death sentence...for you."

Monty was reaching because of what Edith had said, but judging from the split-second of surprise on Ines' face, he had struck a nerve.

"Who said anything about Dexter Montague?" Ines asked, hardening her stare. "He is not the topic of discussion here."

"Isn't he?" Monty asked as he started circling. "Powerful, Archmage or of beyond level of power, has to pose some kind of threat."

"He poses no threat to the High Tribunal."

"I beg to differ," Monty said. "They have tried and failed to get him under control several times in the past. It must irk them to no end that he disregards them so openly."

"He will be brought to account in due time."

"Right. Then there's being partnered to a death goddess, and we know how Verity feels about those."

"Dexter Montague has always had questionable, if not poor, taste in whom he surrounds himself with," Ines said. "Joining with the Morrigan will be his downfall."

"I find that improbable," Monty said. "Unless by downfall you mean she will exhaust him to death from their extracurricular activities?"

"That is *not* what I meant."

"Just checking," Monty said with a curt nod. "Could it be his sudden ascension as head of the Golden Circle? A sect he removed from under the jurisdiction of the High Tribunal without their consent—a sect of battle mages, mind you. That must chafe your elders in the Tribunal, don't you think?"

"As I said, Dexter Montague is not the topic of discussion here."

"Wrong. I'd say he's been the topic of discussion from the moment they sent you after Simon and me. Am I mistaken?"

"Discussion over," Ines said, her expression hardening. "The Tribunal has sanctioned your erasure and Strong's extermination with extreme prejudice."

She lunged forward.

THIRTEEN

Ines was good.

Better than good. She was extraordinary.

Her initial lunge was almost too fast to follow.

Monty parried the thrust and side-stepped her follow-up slash. He narrowly avoided a dagger to the throat that I hadn't even noticed in her opposite hand.

If she was extraordinary, Monty was unnatural. Either he had been practicing, or he had never revealed his true skill with his blades. The Sorrows wailed—the soft cries filling the sub dock and creeping me out—as he parried every attack.

She kept trying to press him but he moved like smoke, avoiding every attack. He wasn't toying with her; I saw the focus on his face. What he was doing was demonstrating his superior skill.

I turned to make sure the *Mobula* was ready to go. Now all we needed was my hellhound and Quan.

Ines thrust with the dagger, following up with a vertical upward slash with her blade. Monty parried the thrust and stepped inside her slash attack, stopping it before it could cut him.

He dematerialized one of his Sorrows and drove a fist into her solar plexus. I heard the *whoosh* of air from where I stood. Ines stumbled back as Monty closed the distance. He struck her chest in several locations with an open palm, covered in violet energy.

Ines opened her eyes in surprise, dropping her blade and falling back to the ground.

"How did you—" she started as she gasped for air. "That attack? He taught *you*? How? You have no right!"

Rage fought with surprise and shock on her face.

"I have every right," Monty said calmly. "You betrayed his trust. You betrayed him."

"So self-righteous," she spat. "I did what I needed to do. What I had to do. Your past is darker than mine."

"Yes. Yes, it is," Monty said. There was a sadness in his voice: regret, and...something else. "He wanted to make sure it wasn't lost."

"How could he? Why would he teach it to *you*?" Ines said, looking down. "Why?"

"Because he feared you would join Verity," Monty said. "He feared you would corrupt its use and his legacy. He was right. He knew you better than you knew yourself. *That* is why he taught me."

"I *will* kill you, Tristan," she said through clenched teeth as she struggled to sit up through the gasps. "I will end you."

"Not tonight," he said, stepping back. "You know the dangers of the Interrupting Palm."

"Don't you dare lecture me on my family technique," she hissed. "*My* father created that technique."

"I know."

"You traitor," she spat. "You should have refused. I'll see you dead for this."

"I advise against any sudden movements," Monty said, calmly stepping back onto the deck of the *Mobula* as he absorbed the other blade. "You and I both know the outcome if you do. You'll need medical attention. I made it a point to avoid your heart...this time. Your lungs are in a state of spasm. Take shallow breaths and you should be fine until you recover."

"You bastard."

"Incorrect," Monty said, looking off to the side suddenly. "I am well aware of my parentage. I do hope this wasn't too boring for you. Next time—"

"Next time, I will burn you all to ash."

"I look forward to your attempt."

Monty stepped to one side of the deck and began gesturing, his hands glowing with golden light. A second later, Peaches tumbled onto the deck where Monty had been standing a moment earlier, covered in blood, alongside a bloody and broken Quan. Monty turned, his focus completely on his injured friend.

I made to run to Peaches, but Monty held up a hand and gave me a head shake.

"It's not his," he said, his voice tight. "It's hers."

"No," I said in a low voice "Will she—?"

"Simon, there are more Blades coming," he said, making Quan comfortable. "This would be a good time for us to exit."

Ines' rage-filled scream filled the sub dock as we pulled away.

FOURTEEN

Once the canopy covered the deck in an airtight seal, I pushed the Mobula under the surface of the water as the radar display appeared on the main screen.

"I'm not a submariner," I said as we left the dock. "Plus, this boat is a snail underwater. Does this thing say twenty knots max?"

"This is a SuNaTran vessel, not a military vehicle," he said. "I doubt the intended use was to outrun angry Verity agents bent on our destruction."

"Doesn't he know us by now?" I asked. "Anything he lends you needs to have an emergency button that allows us to approach the speed of 'oh shit, we're going to die' at any moment."

"You do have a point," Monty agreed. "I'll make sure to pass your sentiment along."

"You do that," I said, tapping the display. "I can run faster than this. We're better off on the—"

"Surface once you clear the island and head north," Monty said without looking up. "Quan doesn't have much time. I can't stop the bleeding effectively and Haven is being watched."

"What's wrong with her?"

"I don't know," Monty said, his voice urgent. "She has been exposed to some kind of poison as best I can assess."

"Where to?" I asked, worried, at the concern in Monty's voice. "Do we have another medical facility close by that can treat her?"

"Not on this side of the island," Monty said. "At least not one that would welcome us willingly."

"Must be that wake of death and destruction that keeps following us around, making us unwanted,' I said. "I'd take it personally if it wasn't true. Where am I headed, then?"

"We need to get to the Cloisters. The *Mobula* should be fast enough to outrun anything Verity throws at us. Cecil is a firm believer in speed over function."

"I really hope you're right," I said, looking at the sonar/radar display again as I navigated our way out of the sub dock. "Looks like we have a welcome committee."

"That would be expected," Monty said, tightly. "I have every confidence in your abilities to evade capture."

Three large ships were docked in the Ellis Island port. I kept the *Mobula* submerged and hoped they didn't have some kind of sonar as we passed under them. Around the three larger boats, I saw a handful of smaller crafts.

"Any chance Verity brought speed boats?" I asked as we moved farther away from Ellis Island. "You know, to prevent us from getting away?"

"Did I mention I'm trying to stop Quan from bleeding out?" Monty snapped. "Hope for the best and—"

"Prepare for the worst," I finished as I surfaced the *Mobula* and began opening her up. "We have incoming."

The five smaller boats had left the dock and were headed our way—fast.

The speedometer on the display changed from twenty to sixty knots once I surfaced. We didn't exceed twenty knots, even though the display was reading a sixty-knot maximum, and I was pushing the Mobula for all she was worth.

I looked around for what I could be missing to increase our speed.

"We need to increase our speed," Monty said. "There are Blades on those boats."

"Thank you, Captain Obvious," I said under my breath. "Going as fast as I can."

"It's not fast enough," he said. "I can't spare any energy over the water to increase our velocity. Go faster."

"Display says sixty knots," I called out, "but we're crawling at twenty still. If you have any ideas, now would be a good time to share."

Sixty knots was blazing for any kind of boat, outside of racing speed boats. Another section of the console opened and I saw a series of three red switches rise from a recessed panel.

A transparent cover prevented the switches from being accidentally engaged. The cover itself read: N_2O—IN CASE OF EMERGENCY in bright red lettering. The switches were numbered from one to three.

Cecil did plan ahead, because unless I was mistaken, these three switches were our "oh shit, we're going to die" velocity-improvement option.

It was still night, which bought us some time. I flipped up the cover and was about to flip the first switch when Monty appeared next to me.

"Did you retract the wings?" he asked, hitting another series of buttons which caused the wings on the side of the *Mobula* to accordion and retract into the hull of the yacht. "If you flip those switches with the wings extended, the force generated by the engine will rip them right off, damaging the integrity of the ship."

"I don't think Cecil would like that," I said as we picked up speed. "That did it, thanks."

He looked down at the switches again.

"It would seem Cecil does know us well," he said. "You may want to start flipping those switches."

"Was just about to, with the wings extended," I said with a small shake of the head. "That would have made our three-hour tour a thirty-second sinking."

"I'm just going to pretend I understand what you're referencing as I try to keep those two safe."

"Isn't that what you usually do?" I asked. "I know it's what I do when you get all magespeaky."

He nodded with a grunt and headed back to Quan and Peaches. I saw him extend his hands covered in golden energy over my hellhound. The blood may not have been his but he was hurt. Every part of me wanted to run over to my hellhound, but I didn't know how to cast healing spells, and Monty did.

Peaches tried to stand and stumbled back onto his haunches. He gave off a low growl, before falling over to his side, his tongue lolling out of his mouth as he panted.

<Hey, boy! What's wrong?>

<My insides hurt.>

My stomach clenched in fear.

<Hurt how? Like you hit the hard door too hard?>

<Hurt like when I ate the bad meat.>

<The meat I made?>

<No. The other bad meat. The one that really hurt me inside.>

He was referring to the time that Thomas poisoned him with meat, nearly killing my hellhound.

This was bad.

<Thank you for being the most amazing hellhound I know and getting the bald lady.>

I was trying my best to keep my voice upbeat and level.

<I am the most superior mighty hellhound you know.>

<Yes, you are. Let me tell Monty what's wrong with you.>

<Can you tell him to make me extra meat? You promised.>

<Let's get your insides better, and then you can have all the extra meat you can eat.>

I heard a mental chuff which meant this plan was starving-hellhound approved.

"I think Edith poisoned him, too," I said, my voice tight with an effort not to scream. "He says his insides hurt like that time Thomas poisoned him."

Monty nodded in agreement.

"I figured something like this would happen," Monty said, moving his golden glowing hands around Peaches' midsection. "It seems to be his only point of vulnerability."

"Poison?"

"His stomach and insatiable appetite," Monty said. "Can you ask him how it happened? I'm certain sausage or meat is involved somewhere."

<Hey, boy. How did you hurt your stomach?>

<I didn't. The smelly lady made me some meat, and it was so good. I was starving and she made me even more. Then I took the bald lady away because the smelly lady hurt her.>

"Nailed it in one," I said to Monty. "Edith gave him tainted meat."

Monty nodded as he intensified the glow around Peaches' midsection.

"That should stabilize him until he can get real attention," he said, wiping the sweat from his brow before heading back to Quan. "We need to go faster."

"How bad is she?"

"I'm a mage not a doctor," he snapped. "Whatever Edith hit her with surpasses my abilities to stop. I can slow it down, but it's spreading through her body. My knowledge is limited to battlefield medicine. I know enough to keep someone fighting without dying in the immediate future. According to my best guess, she has an hour at most, and that's being optimistic."

When Monty was being optimistic, I knew things had gone from bad to horrific. I was about to flip the first switch when a red orb of energy sailed past my head, narrowly missing me.

"What the—?" I said, ducking. "I think they're trying to make a point."

Monty gestured and a golden lattice covered the rear of the Mobula. Another red orb hit it and bounced off, splashing into the water and exploding like a depth charge.

"I can't engage them at the moment," Monty said. "Our best course of action is to go faster and outpace them."

I flipped the first switch and the *Mobula* kicked forward with a roar from the engines. Monty was right—Cecil preferred speed over function. I heard some creaks from the hull as the *Mobula* raced north, but she remained in one piece. The speedboats dropped farther behind as we increased the distance between us.

The Cloisters was situated near Fort Tryon Park. I had just crossed the lower tip of Manhattan, and the island went on for another fourteen miles. I figured The Cloisters were closer to thirteen miles away, give or take a few yards.

Out of the corner of my eye, I saw Monty gesture again. A large golden lattice intertwined with violet energy descended over Quan and Peaches, who lay next to each other. The lattice rested on them, creating a bubble of energy over their bodies.

Monty appeared next to me a few seconds later, looking exhausted.

"I could really use a hot cuppa about now," he said with a short groan. "I've stabilized them both, but it's only a stopgap measure. They're in danger."

We all were.

I reached inside my pocket and handed Monty my flask of javambrosia. He raised an eyebrow and accepted the flask with a nod.

"Sip, don't gulp," I said as he raised the flask to his lips. "That's not a cuppa of anything, but it will energize you."

"I do recall the effects," Monty said. "Thank you for the reminder."

He lifted the flask to his lips and took a small sip before returning it to me. I felt his energy signature increase around us, and the lattice around Peaches and Quan intensified as well.

"That's new," I said. "I don't remember it ever doing that."

"Nor do I," Monty said, flexing his fingers. "It does, however, taste magnificent."

"Think you should let Aria know we're on our way?" I asked, gripping the steering wheel tight. "I recall her not being overly excited about uninvited guests."

"I shall," Monty said. "Once we get closer. Right now, our priority is to focus—"

A white orb of energy shot past us and into the river, showering us with water and raising a wave that shunted us to the side.

"These guys have piss-poor aim," I yelled, swerving to the side as we were drenched. "What are they trying to do? Drown us?"

Monty turned back to look at the speedboats. He flexed his jaw as his expression became grim.

"They aren't trying to hit us directly," he said, moving back to the bubble of protection around Peaches and Quan. "They are attempting to capsize us."

"What? Capsize us?"

"It's when a boat or ship is overturned, rendering it inoperable."

"Thanks for the clarification, Merriam-Webster!" I shouted. "I'm aware of what capsizing is. Can they do it?"

"Displacing enough water in proximity will cause a large enough wave, flipping the *Mobula*, and us," he said, still looking behind us. "It's possible if aimed and timed correctly."

"A simple yes would've been enough."

"That's what I just said: yes," Monty replied with a huff. "It's possible."

"Strap in," I said, putting my finger on the second switch. "We're going to see how much Cecil prefers speed over function."

I felt an energy surge and used a precious second to look back and curse. A volley of large, glowing white orbs launched into the sky behind us and headed our way at speed.

"Evasive maneuvers will be the order of the night," Monty said, strapping in. "I'll try to deflect what I can, but most of my energy is invested in keeping that healing lattice intact."

"I got this."

I nodded and flipped the second switch.

FIFTEEN

I so didn't have this.

The *Mobula* went from blazing subyacht to screaming lightning vehicle in the space of three seconds. The engines shuddered, giving off a high-pitched whine before settling into a throaty rumble.

Another roar filled the night and the engine kicked again, launching us forward even faster. We had left sixty knots behind after I had flipped the first switch.

I had no idea how fast we were going, but I knew we couldn't sustain this speed for long. The faster we went, the straighter I had to keep our path. Usually this was a good idea —except when you had people behind you trying to shoot orbs and who knew what else at you.

That made you an easy and predictable target.

The creaks in the hull were much louder this time as I gently tapped the console.

Hold it together just a little longer. You can do it, girl.

The display lit up with several warnings and exclamation points, detailing different sections of the *Mobula* that were under what—I could only imagine—was immense stress from going faster than any yacht this size should be able to go.

I glanced down at the third switch and really hoped we didn't need it.

The large white orbs crashed into the river behind us, setting off massive depth charge explosions in the water.

"That burst of speed bought us a few seconds," Monty said, standing. "I'm going to alert Aria. Once I do, they will intensify their pursuit."

"You mean it's not intense now?"

"No," Monty said. "They still want to apprehend us. Once that shifts, they will move to a different strategy."

"Which is?"

"Seek and destroy, with emphasis on destroy," he said, looking behind us. "When that happens, you may need to use that last switch."

"I don't think that's a good idea."

"It's a horrible idea," Monty said, gesturing. "It is, however, the only option left. Unless you have a better one?"

"Not at the moment," I said, keeping one eye on the river and another on the display informing me that things on the *Mobula* were NOT GOOD across several systems. "I think if I flip that last switch, we'll have to swim to the Cloisters, if we don't explode first."

"I believe you were the one that requested an 'oh shit, we are going to die' speed option? Seems like Cecil anticipated your wishes."

"It wasn't a literal request," I snapped. "We are way past maxing out the speed at this moment. Do you know what the third switch does?"

"I would imagine it makes us go faster still?"

I glared at him for a split-second, which was all I could spare, considering how fast we were moving.

"Very...scientific...assessment," I said, fighting to keep the wheel straight and the *Mobula* on course. "Maybe we don't need the last switch?"

"Unlikely," Monty said. "They *are* closing on us."

"What?" I asked. "How? Do you realize how fast we're going?"

"Somewhere between bloody and staggeringly," he said, peering into the night. "This should let Aria know we are on our way."

He moved to the front of the yacht and angled an arm up, releasing a large violet orb of energy. It raced forward faster than we were moving, then disappeared into the night.

"What was that?" I asked, looking up as a red beam sliced through the canopy on my right. "Shit! What was *that*?"

"That would be the Blades shifting objectives," Monty said, glancing back as he moved closer to Quan and Peaches. "There will be no questions asked and no quarter given. Our deaths have been sanctioned by the High Tribunal."

"It's good to know where you stand when death is involved," I muttered, holding onto the steering wheel for dear life. "They won't mind if we respond in kind, then, will they?"

"Let's focus on evading, not killing them," Monty said, his voice strained. "We will not debase ourselves to their level of interaction...at least not yet."

"Unless our lives are on the line," I said. "Then I'm not above debasing myself if it means I keep those around me alive."

"Agreed," Monty said. "It would seem they are preparing something especially nasty to send our way. You may want to consider flipping that switch."

I let my finger hover over the switch when I heard and felt an energy surge behind us. It sounded like we had just sped into a Christopher Nolan film. The foghorn of doom hit me with a deep *BRAAAM* that grabbed my attention immediately.

"That didn't sound good," I said. "When attacks have sounds effects like that, it's never a good sign."

I turned to look behind us and saw a large red-and-green orb speeding our way...and gaining.

"That orb is an attack from Ines," Monty said, keeping his gaze fixed on the orb. "She recovered faster than I anticipated."

"Monty," I said. "Do you have a response for whatever that is?"

"Not currently, no," he said. "Not without exposing your creature and Quan."

"You'd better come take the wheel, then," I said, grimly. "I have one idea."

"You have an...? No. Absolutely not, Simon," Monty said. "Your blood is poisoned. We have no idea what could happen if you attempted to use your magic missile."

"What happens if that thing hits us?" I asked. "Because I'm getting serious *Mobula*-melting vibes from that orb."

"I doubt this vessel can survive a direct hit from that orb," Monty said, his voice low as he kept his eyes on the fast-approaching orb of death. "It reads like a disintegrator. One of Ines' signature casts."

"I'm not in the mood to get disintegrated tonight," I said, handing the steering wheel to Monty. "Once I fire my missile, flip the third switch."

Monty shook his head.

"This can go wrong in so many ways," he said, grabbing the wheel and letting one hand hover over the third switch. "I'm ready."

I made my way to the rear of the Mobula, stepping carefully around the prone bodies of Quan and Peaches. My heart constricted when I saw my hellhound sprawled out, having a hard time breathing.

That quickly became rage as I realized that Edith and Verity had tried to kill my hellhound, my bondmate. The rage surged inside me as I extended an arm.

Black energy formed around my arm, laced with red and gold, as sound became muffled around me. In the distance, I could hear Monty calling out my name and yelling at me to stop.

It was too late.

You can attack me, but you never, *ever* touch my hellhound and live to talk about it.

I looked down at my body, now covered in black smoky energy. Arcs of red and gold crisscrossed over my body. Power surged through me—more power than I had ever felt before. It raced through my body, coalescing in my center.

I felt it build and increase inside.

My body flushed with heat as it dealt with whatever was happening to me. I saw the red glow reflecting off the deck and realized distantly the glow was coming from me.

From my eyes.

I turned back one more time and looked at Monty. For the first time, I saw fear in his eyes. It wasn't fear *of* me—it was a fear of what was happening *to* me.

"You have to stop, Simon," he said. "This will kill you."

"Them first," I said, turning back to face the orb trailing behind us. I took a deep breath and braced myself. "*Ignis vitae.*"

SIXTEEN

My first sensation was pain.

Excruciating agony shot up my extended arm. For a few seconds, my vision tunneled in as I nearly lost consciousness. This was the sort of pain that stole your breath and punched you in the throat while you gasped for air.

It had become familiar, which was why I didn't pass out.

I clenched my teeth and kept my arm outstretched as the pain magnified and relocated to my center, before racing out of my arm.

A beam of black, violet, and gold energy shot out of my hand and into the orb behind us, punching through it and blasting it to nothing. The beam didn't stop. It slammed into one of the speedboats, shredding it to splinters, before bisecting a second speedboat behind it.

I was having trouble controlling my arm as the beam continued flowing for a few more seconds. Our pursuers peeled away, giving us space. I still felt the energy inside of me, which was odd.

Usually when I fired a magic missile, the energy would

dissipate after I unleashed the blast. This time, it felt like I was still spooling energy into my body.

I was about to ask Monty what was going on when the energy surged again. My arm burst into black flame and I could feel the skin melting away as the flames consumed me.

My curse couldn't keep up with the damage.

That's when I started screaming.

I felt Monty approach my side, his face grim as he stepped close to my arm.

"This is going to be unpleasant," he said, and gestured. "Brace yourself."

"Are you...are you serious? Brace myself?" I asked, incredulously. "Whatever it is you're going to do...do it...now."

A black-and-green lattice of energy fell on my arm, enveloping it from my finger tips to my shoulder as I sagged to the ground. The burning sensation intensified for a few more seconds as I screamed myself hoarse.

In moments, the pain was suddenly gone.

Along with my arm.

I stumbled back to the deck in shock.

"What did you do?" I asked. "Where is my arm?"

"No time to explain," Monty yelled as he raced back to the pilot's chair and flipped the third switch. "Hold on!"

I found his choice of words ironic, since I currently only had one arm to hold onto anything with. I don't want to say I was getting hysterical, but the thought of spontaneously losing my arm was definitely shrieking through my brain.

He disintegrated my arm? He disintegrated my arm. He disintegrated my arm!

I flexed the fingers on my missing arm. I still had sensation, I just couldn't see my fingers—or arm, for that matter.

Is this what they meant by phantom sensations?

I didn't trust myself to speak, fearing that the only sound I would make would be one long scream. Actually, the next sound I heard was a scream; I had to double check to make sure it wasn't me.

It was the *Mobula*.

Or, more precisely, the two small turbofan engines that protruded from the same space where the wings had extended earlier when the *Mobula* submerged.

The yacht shot forward as the canopy descended on the deck sealing us in. The sudden movement caused me to roll to the rear. The only reason I remained in the yacht was because the canopy had enclosed the deck.

I hung onto one of the deck chairs as the yacht felt like it floated up higher on the water. I managed to look up at a determined Monty, who was gripping the steering wheel in a stranglehold.

The display was counting down from twenty seconds.

As I crawled forward, from chair to chair, the groans from the hull became sharper. Somewhere beneath us, I heard a whip crack and the entire yacht shuddered. If we kept going at this speed, there was no way the yacht would remain intact. I glanced behind us, but didn't see the remaining speedboats.

"Cut the engines!" I yelled. "Before she tears herself apart!"

"I would want nothing more than to be able to stop this engine," Monty yelled back over his shoulder. "But it seems we are locked into the countdown!"

"Did you try turning it off or flipping the switch back?"

"Thank you for that sage advice," he called out as he struggled to hold onto the wheel. "It never occurred to me to flip the bloody switch. What a...novel idea!"

He was scared, which meant I was on the verge of losing it.

I took a deep breath and let it out slow.

A cold calm came over me as I assessed our situation. We

still had about fifteen seconds left on the timer, but the *Mobula* wasn't going to last that long. We needed to retract the turbofans before she broke apart.

The wings.

It was worth a try.

"Engage the wings!" I yelled over the scream of the turbofans. "That should shut down and retract the turbofans."

Monty nodded and pressed some buttons. I really hoped we weren't going too—

"Bloody hell!" he yelled as the engines died down. "Hold on!"

The engines retracted as I expected. Cecil had designed the turbofans for surface travel. Activating the wings, however, prepped the *Mobula* for submersion.

There was only one problem.

We were moving too fast to have the wings extended. They slid out from the sides of the *Mobula,* and for a few seconds we were actually skimming the surface of the river, before both wings tore off with a brutal mangling sound of metal and carbon fiber.

The *Mobula* was still going too fast.

The timer had stopped at five seconds. We were going slower, but it wasn't going to make a difference—we weren't slowing down. Another whip crack sounded under me, louder than the first time, and I saw smoke billow upward from below.

"We're on fire," I said. "We have to abandon ship!"

"Not yet," Monty said, setting his jaw. "The Cloisters is up ahead."

I looked up and saw the Cloisters towering above us.

"That doesn't help us," I said, panic in my voice. "It's up there and we're down here. You plan on flying us up there?"

"We only need to dock," Monty said. "Strap into something. This is going to be an ugly docking procedure."

"Are you insane?" I said, looking at him. "We can't dock at this speed. We'll tear through anything we hit."

"The Inwood Canoe Club has a low stone dock," Monty said. "The columns can stop us."

"*The columns can stop us?*" I repeated. "Holy hell, Monty, have you totally lost it? The columns will shred us to bits if we don't pulverize them first."

"I will try and slow us down somewhat and then I will cast a shield," he said. "We're going to need your dawnward. Do you think you can cast it with one arm?"

I stared at him in disbelief.

"Do we have a choice?" I asked, squatting next to Peaches and Quan, who were still covered by the golden lattice, and using the straps of a nearby chair to tie myself down. "Wouldn't it be easier to cast a lattice over all of us?"

"No, it wouldn't," he said, pointing ahead. "Besides, we're out of time."

I saw the lights that defined the stone dock ahead of us. It was coming at us fast enough to make me reconsider this insane plan and jump off the *Mobula*.

I looked over to the side and seriously thought about how hard the water would feel at this speed.

"It would feel like jumping onto concrete," Monty said, reading my expression. "You're better off riding out the collision in the *Mobula*. If you jumped out, you would still be traveling at high speed, except now, it would just be your body colliding with the water, the columns, and very likely the *Mobula* itself. That would be detrimental to your well-being."

"I would be better off riding out the collision in the Mobula?" I said. "Do you understand how deranged that sentence sounds?"

"I'm aware," he said. "When I divert our course, cast the dawnward."

"Divert the——?"

He pulled on the steering wheel, making a hard right and, turning the Mobula sideways, and aimed us for the rapidly approaching stone dock.

"Now!" he yelled. "Cast it!"

He jumped down from the pilot's chair, and crouched next to me and gestured as he grabbed onto a free strap from another chair. A golden dome descended over us, anchoring us in place. I could see the strain on Monty's face as I focused and materialized the dawnward.

The violet dome of the dawnward was laced with black strands of energy which crisscrossed its surface. It felt like an additional pressure on us, forcing us down into the deck.

It's never looked like that before.

The moment the *Mobula* was perpendicular to the dock, it flipped into the air, tumbling sideways toward the columns supporting the stone dock. We crashed through the first column with a crunch and kept going, blasting through two more before coming to a sudden stop.

The section of the dock we crashed through crumbled into the river behind us, its support gone. Parts of the yacht fell off, sinking into the river next to us. We were right-side up, but water was making its way up to the deck.

"We're taking on water," I said, standing unsteadily as the dawnward and Monty's shield dematerialized. "Remind me to never go boating with you again...ever."

"Grab your creature," he said with a groan. "I'll take Quan."

"How exactly am I supposed to do that?" I said, waving my remaining arm. "With one arm?"

"Your other arm is right there, you just can't see or feel it entirely at the moment," he said. "I'll explain later. Right now, you need to grab your creature. We may have outpaced Verity, but they *are* coming."

I scooped up Peaches. My vanished arm tingled as if I had

slept on it. Pins and needles raced across its length as I winced at the strange sensation.

"This feels bizarre," I said as we left the dying and drowning *Mobula*. "What did you do?"

"Later," he said, carrying Quan across the dock. "We need to get off the water before Verity arrives."

I gave the Mobula one last look before stepping off her deck and onto what was left of the dock.

Thank you for holding on till the very end, girl.

"Cecil is going to lose his mind," I said, looking past the *Mobula* and down the river. "We still have incoming."

In the distance, I could see one large ship headed our way. It was surrounded by three smaller ships, and it looked like they were in a hurry to get to us.

"Hurry," Monty said, leading the way. "Up that road."

The Inwood Canoe Club had a small road that led to Riverside Drive. We followed that for about five minutes before Monty made a sudden right onto another smaller road. The sign read Margaret Corbin Drive and sloped up to the Cloisters.

Monty didn't slow down until we heard the footsteps behind us. Monty placed Quan gently on the grass and I laid Peaches down next to her.

"How did you stop my disintegrator over flowing water?" a voice asked in the darkness.

Ines. A very upset-sounding Ines.

She stepped into view, a black orb in her hand. Around us, more Blades appeared, each of them with a black orb in their hands to match. I looked out to the river, but the ship was still far away.

How did they beat us here?

"You're wondering how we got here so fast," Ines said, looking at me. "You tell me how Tristan neutralized my disintegrator and I'll tell you how we got here before you."

"He can't tell you that," Monty said. "He's not a mage."

"I'm aware," Ines said, giving me a sidelong glance. "Still, he has some basic knowledge. Enough to be dangerous." She turned to Monty. "How did you do it?"

"I used an ancient cast," Monty said. "A nullifier. Your turn. How did you get here before us?"

"You told us where you were going," Ines said, looking up at the Cloisters' Tower. "When you sent that blast, it was easily tracked. The options on this side of the island are limited. Especially when you have injured."

She glanced down at Quan and Peaches with a smile I wanted to wipe off her face—violently. I let my hand drift to Grim Whisper.

"Don't," she warned, looking at me. "Unless you want my first attack to be your hellhound's last."

"You touch him, you die."

"Promises, promises," she said, before turning to Monty. "This little exercise is finished."

"That doesn't explain how you arrived here," Monty said. "You just shared how you knew, not how you arrived here before us."

"Fixed circle on the main ship," she said. "Amplified teleports for river travel."

"Very cutting-edge," Monty said, looking down river. "How did you track us?"

"You were sloppy," Ines said, "and your yacht gave off an enormous energy signature right before it sank."

"The third switch," Monty said, looking at me. "It must have expended a substantial amount of energy to attain that velocity."

"It did," Ines said. "Also? You lied."

"Did I?" Monty said. "When?"

I could tell Monty was stalling—what I didn't know was what he was stalling for.

"A nullifier wouldn't have had that much force," Ines said. "You're not *that* strong. Not even with the lost blood rune you learned. On the river you wouldn't have been able to release that much power."

Monty gave her a mock bow.

"You're right," he said. "*I* wasn't the one who stopped the disintegrator."

"Then who?" she said, looking from him to me. The realization hit her slowly. "No. That's impossible."

"Occam's razor," Monty said. "The simplest solution is the best one. As you said, it would have been impossible for me to unleash that much power over the river."

"This conversation is over," Ines said. "We have you surrounded, outmatched, and outclassed. You either surrender or we bury your remains here. Choose."

"Neither," Monty said as I felt the energy around us intensify. "You would do well to return to your ship now—while you still can."

"You're in no position to give orders," Ines scoffed. "I'm going to enjoy your erasure."

Either she didn't understand what was happening around us or she didn't care. She was so focused on taking us in that she failed to see how each of the orbs the Blades held slowly disappeared.

It wasn't until her own orb vanished with a *pfft* that she looked around, surprised. She stared at Monty.

"What did you do?"

Monty raised his hands slowly.

"All I did was warn you," Monty said then raised his voice. "I would take it as a personal favor if you didn't kill her."

"She will be escorted back to her ship," another voice said from the darkness. "Please proceed to the facility. Aria is expecting you."

Monty bowed as a group of wordweavers appeared around

the Blades. He bent over to lift Quan, but a wordweaver placed a hand on his arm and shook her head. She whispered some words I couldn't make out. A moment later, Quan and Peaches disappeared in a rose-colored teleportation circle.

"We should go," Monty said, nudging me in the side as I remained focused on the circle that disappeared my hellhound. "They will deal with Verity."

"They will *deal* with us?" Ines said, raising her voice as she turned to face some of the wordweavers. "Do you know who we are? We represent Verity. Do you know who that is, what that is?"

"Verity has no jurisdiction on our lands," another wordweaver answered. "You are on wordweaver property. We will allow you to leave alive, as a favor to Mage Montague. Do not test our patience, goodwill, or resolve on this matter."

"Wordweavers?" Ines snarled. "You *dare* obstruct justice?"

"You're welcome," Monty said as we headed off behind another wordweaver, who led the way back to the Cloisters. "I am glad to see you've recovered from my earlier attack. Please give Tana our regards. I'm sure we will see her soon enough."

Ines was about to unleash another tirade when the area filled with rose-colored teleportation circles. In the span of a few seconds, all of the Blades were gone.

"Would it be too much to hope that they were teleported to outer space?" I asked. "Or at the very least, New Jersey?"

"They most likely sent them back to their ship," Monty said, stumbling before I grabbed his arm, preventing a spill. "Thank you. Maintaining those casts over the river was more taxing than I anticipated."

I looked down river at the large silhouette of the ship still heading our way.

"You think they're going to give up?"

"Not if I know Ines," Monty said. "This failure has only

galvanized her resolve. Verity will come for us—wordweaver property or not—they will not accept this outcome."

"You think Aria is going to help us?" I asked as we moved toward the Cloisters. "We didn't exactly part on the best of terms the last time we saw her."

"I certainly hope so," Monty said. "We're running out of options. I now have to somehow explain to Cecil how his subyacht is now sitting at the bottom of the river, after being smashed to bits."

"He's not going to be happy," I said. "If I were him, the next thing I loaned you would be a fist."

"An action he will consider when I give him the news."

"Maybe wait on sharing that for a few days, or years," I said, shaking my head. "Cecil really does believe in speed over function. That yacht felt a need...a need for speed. Maybe if you tell him it saved our lives, he'll take the news better?"

"A small consolation when he will want to kill me," Monty answered. "I'm fairly certain he will suggest I should have gone down with the ship."

"The *Mobula was* a beautiful subyacht."

"It certainly was."

I looked around as we walked along the path that surrounded the Cloisters. Fort Tryon Park was dense with trees, creating a deeper darkness as the leaves blocked the night sky.

I could sense wordweavers all around us as we navigated the path. They moved silently, but their energy signatures were significant.

"Why didn't you let them kill Ines?" I asked. "She wanted to kill you."

"Her father," Monty said. "Rodrigo Santiago was our close-quarters combat instructor at the Golden Circle. He was one of, if not the best, mage when it came to close-quarters fighting, with and without magic."

"I can see how he would be upset if you dusted his daughter."

"He died some time ago," Monty said, his voice tinged with sadness. "He created and taught me the Interrupting Palm on one condition."

"That you only use it for the forces of good?"

"You've watched too many movies," Monty said after a pause. "He made me vow to never take his daughter's life if she became part of Verity. I should have paid more attention to him."

"Why?"

"Whenever he mentioned Verity, I dismissed his statements as the angry ravings of a concerned father," he said. "We, I...never thought Verity was real."

"They seem pretty real to me," I said. "That orb Ines threw our way seemed pretty real too."

"It most certainly was, that was his fear, that she would join them."

"Which she did," I said. "How did he know she would join them?"

"It was the most probable outcome considering her temperament and view on life and magic," he said. "Ines is very black and white; there is no gray with her. Mages with that mindset can make prime candidates for a group like Verity. They would be actively sought after to join their ranks. Mind you, prior to our recent interactions with them, I thought Verity was a myth."

"Something made up to keep mages in line?"

"Something like that, yes," he admitted. "At best, we thought it was a fringe group made up to threaten young mages. Not an actual worldwide organization."

"Behave or the Mage Police will get you sort of thing?" I said, shaking my head. "After meeting Cain and Edith...fringe fits."

"At the very least, no one ever believed the rumors about them," he said. "I certainly didn't."

"Yet here we are, facing off against the very real myth," I said. "I take it her father was less than pleased?"

"He was livid," Monty said. "He disowned her and cast her from his home."

"A little harsh, don't you think?"

"Not for him. Actually, I'm surprised he didn't erase her himself," Monty said. "He hated everything Verity stood for with a passion."

"Is that when he taught you the Interrupting Five Point Palm Exploding Heart Death Touch?"

"There's no such thing," he answered, giving me a look. "To answer your question, yes, that is when he taught me the Interrupting Palm, made me promise not to mortally injure her with it, and if possible, get her out of Verity...alive."

"That last part is going to be a tough one, I think. She drank all the Verity Kool-Aid. Third-in-command of the Blades? No way you're getting her out of there alive."

"We'll see," Monty said. "Stranger things have happened."

I looked up at the hill we still had to climb. A soft groan escaped my lips and I immediately felt exhausted. It didn't help that the wordweavers around us were moving effortlessly, with not even a stumble or a single instance of shortness of breath among the bunch.

"Is there any reason why we aren't getting the teleportation treatment?" I asked curiously. "I mean, smashing a yacht through stone columns only sounds fun on paper. Not so much in real life."

"They can't teleport you," Monty said. "Part of you is in-between." He pointed at my invisible arm. "It would disrupt your energy signature further, and you are already poisoned. The risk of permanent damage is too great."

"Oh," I said. "That explains me. Why aren't they teleporting you?"

"My prolonged casting over the river taxed my defenses," he said. "Teleportation would have an adverse reaction on my body in this state."

"How adverse?"

"You recall your digestive destruction after every teleport?"

"Do I have to?"

"Imagine that times ten."

"Are you *sure* they can't teleport you?" I asked. "You look absolutely exhausted."

"Your concern is moving, but I'll walk, thank you."

SEVENTEEN

After what felt like a lifetime—but was probably closer to fifteen minutes—we arrived at the home of the wordweavers.

The absolute peace of the place never failed to amaze me. I saw the pink of the sun as it brightened the horizon. At the sight of the new dawn, I actually let out a sigh of relief.

The wordweavers led us to a large room with two large beds.

"I need to see my hellhound," I said. "He's been poisoned."

The wordweaver who led us to the room nodded her head, but didn't budge. I looked at Monty.

"Does she understand English?" I continued under my breath. "I'm not going to take a nap until I know how he is."

"Your bondmate is being healed," the wordweaver said. "As is your other companion. Aria requests that you rest before meeting."

"Rest?" I asked, upset. "Did you not hear what I said? My hellhound, my bondmate, has been poisoned. I need to see him—now."

"You will see him soon," she said. "First, you must rest."

I made to push my way past her when she whispered something in my ear. My legs suddenly felt heavier and my eyes started closing against my will.

"What...what did you do?" I asked, turning to her and slurring my words. "I need to...need to go...Peaches."

The room became black after that.

****

The sun blazed in my eyes when I opened them. Monty stood by my bed with a steaming mug of Earl Grey in his hand. The wordweaver who had whispered in my ear stood by the door, looking at me with a peaceful smile on her lips.

I scowled in response.

"You're awake. Good," he said after taking a sip. "She's waiting for us."

"Coffee?" I asked, eyeing his mug. "Would it be too much to ask?"

"Of course not," Monty said, motioning to a small table beside the bed with his mug. A large mug of inky javambrosia called to me. "I took the liberty of preparing a close approximation of your Deathwish."

I grabbed the mug and took a long pull. A groan of satisfaction escaped my lips as the coffee goodness flooded my system.

"How long was I out?" I asked, giving the wordweaver by the door plenty of stink eye. "How did she knock me out?"

"A few hours," Monty said, nodding to the wordweaver. "She's a wordweaver. I would imagine she used a word of power to induce sleep."

"That was cheating," I said. "She could have asked, you know."

"What would she have asked?" Monty said. "You were

determined to see your creature. You didn't listen, so she facilitated the rest you sorely needed."

I took another pull from the mug and set it down on the table.

I stretched my arms and then looked down in surprise as my invisible arm was no longer invisible. It was still covered in black and green energy but it didn't feel full of pins and needles.

"My arm is back," I said, looking down at it and flexing my fingers. "Thanks."

"It was never gone," Monty said. "Don't thank me. It was her."

Monty motioned to the wordweaver in front of us.

"Thank you," I said, raising my hand and giving Monty a sidelong glance. "I prefer to be able to see both of my arms."

"You are welcome," she said, looking at Monty for a moment. "The solution was simple but effective. I'm certain Aria can help you further. Shall we go? She is waiting."

"Indeed," Monty said. "Ready?"

The wordweaver turned and led us out of the room. We followed close behind as we walked the brightly lit corridors. I thought back to the last time we had spoken with Aria.

It wasn't a pleasant memory.

She had been willing to risk the entire city, over eight million people, when William, Monty's older, slightly deranged brother—was trying to form the Gray Heart. To do that, he was going to need to activate a sequence unleashing the Black Heart.

There was one major problem.

At the time, the Black Heart had been in the Fordey Vault, which was ten stories beneath Grand Central...*the* Grand Central, in the middle of *my* city.

Aria had given him the right sequence, but the wrong trigger, in the hopes that he would obliterate himself. The downside was the small detail of that turning the city into a magical wasteland, killing everyone in it.

Monty and I didn't agree on her solution. We had words with her. Unpleasant ones.

She stood on principle—the needs of the many, in this case, the overall population of the planet, outweighing the needs of the few. If you could consider the eight million in the city, the few. I always found this saying was used when the person doing the deciding managed to be part of the many, not the few.

Monty and I found another solution that didn't involve vaporizing an entire city full of people. With the help of Karma, we managed to save the city and stop William.

We didn't exactly leave Aria on the best of terms.

The wordweaver led us through the maze of corridors, each one looking identical to the one we'd previously used. The corridor was featureless stone.

I saw no distinguishing markers or symbols. We walked in silence for a few minutes. When we reached a T-junction, I looked left and right, noticing that all the corridors looked the same.

This went on for another ten minutes until I was completely turned around and lost. Then I recalled that we were walking through the original Corridors of Chaos.

They were designed to be an extensive and complicated network of corridors with shifting and disappearing sections. Not the kind of place you'd want to get lost in. I made sure to stay close to the wordweaver as she navigated the maze.

She made a sharp right that led down a short corridor. At the end of this hall, I saw bright sunlight and a wide glass door which led to a large patio high above ground level.

Once we were outside, I took a moment to appreciate the view.

It was impressive.

I could see the softly glowing runic defenses of the Cloisters shimmering in the air, and stone around the property. The south face looked down into the lush green of Fort Tryon Park. To the west was the Hudson River and a sheer drop into the water.

I shuddered as I looked at the river, remembering our adventure from the night before. A feeling of sadness settled over me as I thought about the *Mobula,* now sitting at the bottom of the Hudson.

Behind us, and to the north, stood the Cloisters Tower: the headquarters for the wordweavers. A small stone path led up to the tower from where we stood on the patio.

The wordweaver led us up even higher until we stood on the summit of a small mountain that was covered in grass and shrubbery. Surrounded by pink marble columns sat a large outdoor courtyard, and in its center, I could see a large pool of clear water.

Next to the pool, another pathway led down the mountain. The woman sitting in front of the pool faced us, but kept her eyes closed. I recognized the intense energy signature around her.

Aria.

"Tristan," she began, with her eyes still closed as we drew near, "I expected—considering your propensity for questionable casts and the influence of your uncle—that it was only a matter of time before Verity set their sights on you. However, Simon attracting their attention is somewhat of a surprise."

Even after all this time, it wasn't hard to believe that Aria was one of the most powerful mages on the planet. She sat in a lotus position, as still as the water in the pool, which reflected the clear blue sky.

"Well met," Monty said with a slight bow. "Once again, we are in need of your assistance."

He gave me a look that said, *This would be a good time to show the appropriate manners.*

"Well met," I said, getting up to speed before he used an elbow on my ribs. "It's good to see you again."

Aria remained seated and opened her eyes. Her long black hair cascaded behind her as she took us in. We must have looked like death warmed over.

"You both look the worse for wear," she said. "Please sit." We sat on the low small benches near the pool. I let out a groan as I squatted low on the bench, my body protesting the sudden bending of my legs. Monty shot me a glance and shook his head. I made no apologies; after last night, I felt close to a hundred years old.

Whatever my curse was doing, healing me back to full strength was not a priority. I groaned again as I shifted into a better position and focused on Aria.

I know I felt and looked like I had been chewed up and spit out a few times. Even with the few hours' rest, my body felt mauled and beaten to a pulp.

My curse had been working overtime just to fight the poison, much less heal any of the injuries I so generously added on our boat trip from hell.

I imagined Monty felt close to the same, having to cast over the river like he did for so long in an effort to keep us in one piece.

"Thank you," I said, once my body found a position I could sit in without feeling immediate pain. "This place is very zen. Can we stay here for a few days or years?"

"I'm afraid not," she said. "You both have very busy lives. Perhaps in a few centuries, when you retire."

"A few centuries?" I asked. "The way things are going, that sounds unlikely."

"Did you have a good nap, Simon?"

I bit back my first response. Aria could probably launch

me over the edge of the west wall and into the Hudson River with a word. Considering my night, it wasn't a trip I had any intention of taking.

"It was a good nap," I said after a pause. "I really would like to go see my hellhound now."

"I know," she said with a small smile. "If you search your bond, you will know he is out of any immediate danger."

I felt for my bond and there it was: a strong sense of Peaches several levels below me. She was right, he felt...steady and hungry. It was the only way I could describe it. His presence was solid. I sensed that he noticed my searching for him. I felt a mental chuff, and then he settled back into a restful state.

I glanced at Aria, let out a sigh of relief, and nodded, which she returned.

She wore her usual white robe covered in silver runic brocade. The silver brocade designated her level of power. After Dahvina, Aria was the most powerful wordweaver on the planet. Unlike Dahvina, Aria's eyes lacked irises, and shone with latent power, making her gaze unnerving at best.

She remained silent for close to thirty seconds, just sitting there and staring. Under normal circumstances, I would have mentioned that we didn't come here for a staring contest. I figured, considering how we left things the last time, that my comment wouldn't be appreciated.

I was learning.

"Thank you for taking care of Peaches," I said, breaking the silence. "We, I, need your help."

"Well met," she said when she was done staring. "I'm afraid that won't be possible."

EIGHTEEN

Her words took me off guard for a few moments.

I was about to respond when she raised a hand and spoke again.

"I can't help you," Aria said as she sat beside the pool, staring at us. "It's not that I don't want to. It's that I *can't*."

"But," I blurted out, "Peaches and Quan, they're both—"

"Fine," she said. "That is not the help I'm referring to. They will be attended to and restored. In fact, Quan is mostly recovered. She is White Phoenix, after all."

"Simon's poison," Monty said, pensively. "You can't reverse it, can you?"

She shook her head.

"If I, or any of the wordweavers, attempted to undo the damage," she said, looking at me, "we would do more harm than good. I can, however, address...that."

She pointed at the lattice of energy around my arm.

"This is an elegant yet simple solution, Tristan," Aria continued, gesturing with one hand. Silver runes floated over to my arm, falling softly on the lattice and unraveling it. "You shifted his arm in-between by merging a teleportation circle and the...Interrupting Palm?"

"Yes," Monty said with a nod. "It seemed like the best solution at the time. We were under attack and I lacked the time to address the situation effectively."

"I was not aware you knew the Interrupting Palm technique," Aria said. "I was under the impression Mage Santiago had vowed never to impart the technique to anyone after his daughter defected to Verity."

"That was his initial position, yes," Monty said. "He changed his mind after much reflection. I was fortunate enough to receive instruction at his hand. I was his last student."

"Tragic but understandable," Aria said. "Did he place conditions on your acquiring the technique?"

"No lethal harm is to come to Ines using his technique, and I am to remove her from Verity alive if possible."

"She is Tana's second," Aria said, with a shake of her head. "Third-in-command in the Blades. Extricating her from Verity will be challenging."

"I am aware it will be difficult," Monty said. "I do have a plan."

"It will need to be ingenious and creative," Aria said "Verity agents rarely, if ever, leave the organization...alive, that is."

"I promised her father," Monty said. "I will do everything possible to make sure she does."

"If she wants to leave at all," Aria said, still looking at my arm as she focused on me. "Please take a deep breath, Simon. This next part will be somewhat uncomfortable."

She whispered a word under her breath and flipped her wrist. Black, violet, and gold energy shot out from my arm and into the air in the shape of a large orb, around a foot in diameter.

Pain shot through my arm as I clenched my teeth. She and I had different definitions of uncomfortable. My breath came in short, ragged gasps as the energy flowed out of me. With another gesture, the orb floated over to her side. She touched it with a finger, then rested a palm on its surface.

"I don't think that's a good idea," I said, warily. "That combination of energy turned out to be volatile last night."

"I'm aware," Aria said, still focused on the orb. "Thank you for the warning. Your concern is noted."

I figured it was the polite thing to do. She may have been one of the most powerful wordweavers on the planet, but I didn't want her facing any nasty surprises because of me or the energy in my body.

I wasn't looking to make any new enemies.

I had enough old ones.

"I can see why Verity has chosen to target you," she said. "It's not just the poison in your blood that they fear, although that is formidable."

"Not exactly the word I would use," I said. "Is the black part the poison in my system?"

"Partly. The violet is part of your base energy and the gold... Hmm... The gold is new," she said, cocking her head to one side. "You've been imparted necromantic knowledge?"

"Something like that, yes."

I explained about Orethe and what she did to Ebonsoul.

"You truly are a mystery, Simon Strong," she said, shaking her head with a slight smile. "This is why Verity would prefer you removed. You are not a mage."

"Not like I've heard that before," I said. "I realize I'm not—"

"No, what you are is much more dangerous, and more potent," she said, lowering her voice. "Verity is trying to remove you before you achieve your potential."

"Why?" I asked. "Why would they feel threatened by me?"

"What concerns them is the merging of these energies, this power. If you somehow managed to harness this"—she tapped the orb and it floated gently over to the pool, hovering above the water—"they would be hard pressed to stop you without the High Tribunal taking an active role."

"We don't want that," Monty said. "That would escalate the conflict."

"Yes...yes, it would," Aria said. "Your uncle would certainly get involved then. He can be something of a blunt instrument when his family is involved. It would not go well for them."

I shuddered at the memory of Nemain.

She made another gesture, and the orb sank into the pool, transforming the water into an inky black liquid with undertones of violet and gold. It bubbled and splashed as if it was boiling. Aria whispered something else I couldn't decipher, and the water immediately cleared, becoming still again.

"Monty thinks Verity is after us because of his uncle," I said. "Is this true?"

"Dexter Montague is a difficult man to understand," Aria said with a tight smile. "He does not respond well to threats, and they have made their intentions clear regarding his use of power."

"They openly threatened Dex?"

"They strongly voiced their opposition to his activities," she said. "Then they overstepped their bounds by sending the Blades after him. This was long before Cain. Verity is an ancient institution."

"What happened to the Blades they sent?" I asked, surprised. "I can't believe they would threaten Dex. Were they suicidal?"

"This was long ago, when Dexter was a young man. Even then, he was a force to be reckoned with."

"That sounds like it didn't go well."

"It did not go well," Aria said. "Dexter sent the Blades back to the High Tribunal in a considerably worse condition than when they arrived. Then he paid the High Tribunal itself a visit."

"He *what*?" I asked, looking at Monty. "Did you know about this?"

Monty shook his head.

"There are many things about my uncle that are hidden from me."

"With good reason, and for your own safety," Aria said. "In any case, he paid the Tribunal a visit." She shook her head. "The High Tribunal is a group of five Archmages considered to be the most accomplished in their disciplines."

"Five Archmages?" I asked in awe. "He went up against five Archmages?"

"No one knows what transpired in that closed meeting," Aria continued. "The Tribunal has never spoken of it and there is no written record. As far as anyone knows, it never happened."

"I've never heard anything about this," Monty said. "I thought the catalyst for Verity was the separation of the Golden Circle. You're saying this goes beyond that?"

"I am."

"How do *you* know it happened?" I asked. "This was a secret meeting."

"I only know of it because *my* master wordweaver instructor acted as a neutral witness to the meeting."

"Did she tell you what happened?"

"No. Never. She was sworn to secrecy and she never broke her vow, taking that secret with her into death," Aria said. "I do know it must have been a significant display of power on

Dexter's part. A truce was brokered during that meeting which has not been tested until the present."

"He convinced five Archmages to leave him alone?"

"That is an oversimplification, but yes," Aria said. "That was the status quo until recently."

"Until he removed the Golden Circle from the body of sects," Monty said. "He became an active threat to the High Tribunal."

"They never forgave him for what occurred in that initial meeting," Aria said with a nod. "He challenged their authority. It was a loss of face for them, and you know mages—egos as fragile as eggshells. Many of them harbored ill-will toward Dexter and the Montagues since that day."

"Toward Dex *and* his family?" I said, glancing at Monty. "It seems they are holding a grudge and taking it out on Monty, too."

"Sadly, yes," she said. "Attacking Tristan is a de facto attack on Dexter. It sounds petty except that this grudge can have lethal consequences if not addressed. Which brings us back to *you*."

"To me?" I asked. "What does this have to do with me?"

"Your actions and the power you wielded last night directly ties you to Tristan and his use of a lost elder blood rune," she said. "Being connected to Tristan directly ties you to Dexter. Verity knows what happened in London with Cain. Your presence there implicates you."

"Implicates me?" I said. "Even though I wasn't the one who neutralized Cain?"

"You stood against Verity and wielded energy against them," she said. "A direct violation of the tenets they uphold. Think of it as attacking the mage police. The moment you stood with Tristan, you became an adversary. After last night, neutralizing the disintegrator, you became an enemy—one to be neutralized and eliminated."

"I don't understand," I said. "I'm no threat to them. I could barely control my power last night. If it wasn't for Monty, I probably would've sliced myself in half with that energy."

"I know," she said. "I'm surprised your arm is still attached to your body after that blast. Tristan's quick thinking saved you."

"Thank you," I said, looking at Monty. "I do appreciate it."

He waved my words away.

"You would have done the same for me," he said and focused on Aria. "This is not connected to removing his poison. Why can't you help him? Isn't it a simple matter of cleansing his blood like you did the water?"

"Tristan," she said shaking her head. "You should know that nothing is ever as simple as it appears. This is not a simple toxin. This is runic poisoning on a scale few have seen or survived. The energy in his body has merged with his blood. To remove the toxin, we would need to remove his blood...all of it. Then we would replace it with new blood, without his body going into shock and killing him."

"Someone already made the offer to remove all of my blood. Pass."

"You're referring to Edith Alnwick," Aria said. "I'm not surprised she's involved in this somehow. She can sense poison, and your blood is a beacon to her right now. If you've attracted Verity, you've attracted Edith. A dangerous enemy indeed."

"Wonderful," I said with a small groan as I shifted on the bench. "Another enemy out to remove me from circulation."

"You do make impressive enemies," Monty said. "Most of them are insane, but impressive nonetheless."

"Should we run down the list of the Squash Mage Montague Club?" I asked. "*Your* enemies span generations."

Monty gave me a look, but remained silent.

"What exactly did she want with you?" Aria asked. "Did she share her intentions?"

"She was pretty focused on my making a full blood donation to the bank of deranged venomancers," I said. "She wants to create the Dragons Breath. Says she can do it with my blood."

Aria shook her head.

"She has always been unstable," she said. "But now her goal may be within reach—with your blood."

"You mean she can really create the super toxin?"

"She is a master venomancer," Aria answered. "She may not be entirely sane, but when it comes to poisons, she is brilliant. If she says she can create it with your blood, I would take her at her word and act accordingly."

"Act accordingly," I said. "As in wipe Verity off the map?"

"That's a little dark, Simon," Monty said, narrowing his eyes at me. "How about we refrain from the wholesale eradication of a group of mages as an option?"

"That would solve nothing," Aria added. "It certainly wouldn't remove the toxin from *your* body."

"But it would definitely make me feel better," I said, without thinking. "Sorry... I must be exhausted. I'm just tired of having a target on my back all the time."

"I understand," Aria said, giving me a glance I couldn't decipher. "No one enjoys being hunted, and right now, Verity is hunting you both."

I nodded, taking in the tranquility of the surrounding courtyard. I took a deep breath and tried calming my thoughts. Something was off. All I wanted to do was take the fight to Verity. I wanted to unleash an ultimate magic missile of death and blast them all off the face of the earth.

I refocused on the problem at hand.

"Are you saying you're not equipped to remove the toxin?" I asked, looking for a solution. "Maybe we can go to Haven?"

"They won't be able to help you there, either," Aria said. "It's not a matter of the tools. If any wordweaver tried to undo your runic poisoning, it would result in an erasure for them. That's how strong it is in your body."

My frustration grew as I clenched my fists. I really thought she would be able to help. Like Monty had said, we were running out of options. Now it seemed like our last option had evaporated right in front of us.

"You said wordweavers, right?" I said, having a moment of clarity. "What about another kind of magic user? Not a wordweaver."

"You mean aside from the venomancer who is looking to remove all the blood from your body?" she asked. "That *would* solve your problem."

"Yes, I'm not really crazy about *her* solution to my problem."

"How much time does he have?" Monty asked, keeping his voice low as he focused on the still water in the pool in front of us. "The blast last night...the scale of power. He dismantled a disintegrator orb with little to no effort—on a flowing river."

"That is quite the feat," Aria said, giving me the once over. "Are you sure there are no mages in your bloodline?"

"Not that I'm aware of."

"That level of power..." Monty mused. "Was his magic missile enhanced by the poison?"

"And the necromancy," Aria said. "Your siphon has been transformed, which means *you* have been transformed."

"Transformed?"

"It's ironic that someone who has difficulty dying would be bonded to a siphon of necromancy within his body," Aria said. "You are a series of paradoxes."

"My entire life is currently a paradox," I said. "What does it mean that I was able to blast the melting orb last night?"

"It means the poison has advanced considerably," Aria said, her expression grim. "I would say you have three to five days before the onset of the final transformation. No more than five days. Less, if you use energy like you did last night."

"Five days?" I asked, as my heart fell into my stomach. "Please tell me there is another solution that doesn't include wordweavers."

"Yes," she said, gazing at the both of us. "You two share a stormblood forged in power and blood. *That* is your solution."

I turned the words over in my head, but they didn't make sense.

"Can you give me the Magic for Dummies explanation?" I asked, still clueless. "How is the stormblood a solution?"

"If you can initiate it, there is a chance it can clear the poison from your system without killing you," she said. "However, the risk to Tristan is considerable. He can face a full erasure of his abilities."

"How large a risk?"

"It would require that Tristan cross lines he has never crossed before. It could potentially cause an erasure that will sever his ability to control and manipulate energy —permanently."

"Will it save him?" Monty asked. "*Can* it save him?"

"Possibly," she said after a few moments. "The alternative, is potentially, a dark immortal."

"That's what Ines called me," I said. "A dark immortal. She said I could be the next one."

"If the poison continues to corrupt you, as it is doing right now, eventually you could transform into one," she said. "It is very rare, but it has happened in the past."

"How often?"

"Often enough that it must not be allowed to occur again

—ever," she said, her voice and expression hard. "The last time a dark immortal walked this plane was over two centuries ago."

"Kana," Monty said. "It took the collective might of several sects to face her. Even then, her death…"

"Her death sparked the Supernatural War," Aria finished. "I will not allow that transformation. Nor will certain other beings on this plane. It poses too much of a threat to the balance."

"What are you saying?" I asked, confused and angry. "I'm not corrupted."

"No?" she asked, with the hint of a smile across her lips. "Who was it that undid the disintegrator last night? Tristan?"

Monty remained silent, but shook his head.

"Then I have to assume it was you," Aria said, turning back to me. "What cast did you use?"

There was no point in lying. She had felt the energy signature from here while we were miles away.

"My magic missile," I admitted reluctantly. "My *uncorrupted* magic missile."

"A magic missile," she said, staring at me with those irisless eyes. "How complex do you think that cast is?"

"Not very, I would guess," I said. "I mean, if I can do it, it can't be too complicated."

"Tell me," she said, looking to one side, "from where does your magic missile derive its energy?"

I really didn't like where this conversation was headed, but I had no choice but to continue. It was similar to slowing down to look at a car crash. You knew it was bad, but you couldn't help staring, thankful that it wasn't you in that mangled vehicle.

"My life force," I said. "It uses my life force."

"Which would make it a potent weapon utilized by an

immortal, considering the abundance of life force you possess, wouldn't you say?"

"I would, yes."

"In the past, when you fired your magic missile—one of the simplest casts available—did it possess the power to neutralize energy?" she asked. "For example, could it undo a disintegrator, like you did last night on a body of flowing water?"

"Not to my knowledge, no."

"That doesn't mean he's being corrupted," Monty said. "It could mean—"

"I'm not finished," she said, cutting him off, before turning back to me. "What color was the beam last night?"

"Black, violet, and gold."

"Like the energy I removed from your arm earlier?"

"Yes, the same colors."

"What color has it always been?"

"Violet," I said, realizing that it was sounding worse by the second. "Is it really *that* bad?"

"Tell me, Simon," she said gently, pointing at my face, "do your eyes usually glow red?"

"Not normally, no," I said, looking down into the pool and seeing my reflection. My eyes were pulsing a dull red. I looked like my hellhound, before he released a baleful glare. "It's bad, isn't it?"

She nodded slowly and gave me a sad look.

"Actions and consequences," she said, holding a hand palm up, then turning it over. "Cause and effect."

"Five days?" I asked. "Five days before I turn into a dark immortal?"

"You are doing no such thing," Monty said, his words clipped. "There is another solution."

"There is," Aria said. "You only need to pay the cost."

"No," I said, glancing at Monty. "That's too risky. Is there another, non-erasure option possible?"

"I'm afraid not," Aria said. "There is a cost, and it must be paid. Always."

"Then no," I said. "I don't want Monty risking his magic to save me. He's a mage. Losing his magic is the worst possible thing that could happen."

"Not the worst," he said. "If you turn into a dark immortal—"

"What?" I asked, warily. "I'm sure Aria could keep me in some secure location so I wouldn't hurt anyone. Right? Maybe I could become the first male monkweaver? You do have a dungeon here, don't you?"

She stared at me for a few seconds and shook her head.

"No," she said. "We would be forced to end your existence."

"We?"

She glanced over at Monty.

Then I knew what would be worse than losing his magic: Monty would have to help eliminate me before I became a full dark immortal.

"There is another way," a voice said from behind us. "It's risky, but safer than a complete erasure for Tris."

It was Quan.

NINETEEN

Quan approached the pool, bowed to Aria, and then sat on the floor, facing her in one graceful movement, making it look effortless, as if she had floated down to the marble edge of the pool.

I turned to her suddenly, hopeful for any option that didn't involve stripping Monty of all his abilities.

"What is this option?" I asked, trying not to sound too hopeful.

"A nexus purifier," Quan said. "He would have to cast the world-ender."

My hopes, which dared to believe we had found a solution, crashed and burned in spectacular Michael Bay style at the mention of a world-ender.

I took a deep breath and slowly exhaled. There had to be a positive spin to this. Just because it was called the world-ender didn't mean the world had to end when it was cast. Did it? I mean, what would be the point of creating a cast you could only use once?

"The nexus purifier isn't strong enough to deal with

Simon's condition," Aria said, crushing me even further. "The poison is too advanced."

"Alone it isn't, but Tris has mastered the lost elder rune of *sealing*," Quan said. "They also share a stormblood. Using the Rule of Three, if you combine elements of all three casts. It can work."

"The Rule of Three?" I asked. "What's the Rule of Three?"

"Catalyst, cleansing, and containment," Quan explained. "We have all three components—storm blood, nexus purifier, and sealing. It can work."

"Or completely undo this plane," Aria countered. "The risk is too great."

"Even here?" Quan asked, defiantly. "The runes containing this place are stronger than any I have seen. With reinforcement, it can be done here."

"You have no idea what you are proposing," Aria said, and turned to Monty. "Is this true? You have mastered the elder rune of sealing?"

"I wouldn't exactly say *mastered*," Monty said, looking at Quan. "I am proficient enough to cast it consistently. I do not, however, know the nexus purifier cast."

"But you could learn it," I said, trying to sound optimistic without sounding optimistic. "I mean, how hard can it be?"

"Immensely hard," Monty said. "As in taking more than five days to learn the rudimentary aspects of the cast hard. Then there's the matter of the blood."

"The blood?" I asked, not liking where this was going. "What blood?"

"The elder rune of sealing is a *blood* rune," Monty clarified. "It requires blood when performed on its own. Combined with the two other casts, I can only assume the blood cost would be significantly higher—that is, if we can even combine the three."

"You don't need to learn the nexus purifier," Quan said. "I know it."

"Can they really be combined?" I asked, daring to hope again. "Will it work?"

"It can," Quan said, confidently. "The elder rune seals, the nexus purifier removes the poison, and the stormblood can power the cast. They can work in conjunction."

"Or blow up the planet?" I asked. "Because that really sounds like a recipe for planetary obliteration."

"It could undo the plane, not the planet," Quan corrected. "The risk of total erasure is less to Tristan than the alternative."

"Oh, *just* the plane? I feel so much better now."

"It's better than the formation of a new dark immortal," she said.

I agreed but was still wary of blowing up the plane with something called the world-ender. When a cast is named after the destruction of the world, I figured it wasn't hype.

"What would I have to do?" I asked, not believing I was actually agreeing to something that could jeopardize the entire plane. "I mean, *if* we could pull this off safely."

"Tristan would cast the rune of sealing. I would have to perform the nexus purifier," Quan said, giving me a look. "You...you would have to start the cast by initiating a stormblood while Aria contained it all in one place. Preferably a place of power."

"Catalyst, cleansing, and containment," I said. "I'm the catalyst?"

"Not *you* exactly—the stormblood," Quan corrected. "The power of that cast is the catalyst."

"Initiate a stormblood?" I said. "I can barely cast a magic missile with this poison in me. When I do, it's on overdrive and out of control. This is insane. I don't know how to initiate a stormblood."

"You can learn," she said, her voice grim. "I can teach you the blood lessons."

"Which will do what exactly?"

"Allow you to channel the energy of the stormblood in your body, at least for a short time," she said. "Long enough to catalyze the cast."

"What happens if we fail?" I asked. "What happens if I turn into a dark immortal?"

"That would be undesirable," Aria said. "If that happens, our options are—limited."

"The poison is only affecting your abilities right now," Quan said. "In time, it will affect your mind. Any moral compass you possess will be subverted. You will take actions that may seem correct to you, but will be abhorrent to everyone you know. You *will* become evil."

"I'm going to become *evil*? Really?" I asked in disbelief. "Isn't that a little much? I'm not evil now. How do I all of a sudden *become* evil?"

"Usually it's a matter of incremental steps," Aria said. "The first life you take is devastating, the second not as much...and the tenth? It barely registers above the rationale 'it is for the greater good'. It happens slowly, imperceptibly."

"I still think it's a stretch to say I'm going to become evil."

"Is it?" Quan asked. "Verity is trying to kill Peaches and all of you. What do you think our response should be?"

Rage flared in my mind. They'd poisoned my hellhound, my bondmate, chased me up the river in an effort to kill us. The only thing they deserved was a long, painful death.

"Death," I said, my voice low and unrecognizable, even to me. "They dared to touch those close to me."

Quan raised an eyebrow.

"Is that the only response?"

Yes... No.

We could neutralize them somehow, without killing them. But they deserve death. All of them. All of them? Yes...all of them.

Kill them all, but make them suffer first.

I shook my head to clear my thoughts.

There had to be another way.

Quan and Aria were right. The poison *was* corrupting me.

"No," I said, after some hesitation. "It's already happening, isn't it?"

Quan nodded.

"If you become a dark immortal," Quan said, "it won't just be Verity after you. Every organization, every group, along with several gods, will step forward to destroy you."

"Destroy?" I asked. "Isn't that a bit extreme?"

"You present too great a threat, especially with your hellhound."

"What happened to peaceful dialogue?" I asked. "Tact and diplomacy? Finding a way to settle differences without bloodshed?"

She gave me a hard stare.

"What did you think would happen?" Quan asked. "A dark immortal is a threat. You would upset the balance and throw everything into chaos. They would be *forced* to destroy you."

There was that word again—chaos.

"What about Kali?" I asked. "Isn't she considered a dark immortal? Maybe she can reverse this?"

"Maybe she can," Quan said, nodding. "Would you like to wait for her help? I'm sure Verity would be understanding. In fact, why don't you reach out and summon her? Do you have a Marked One special-access prayer? Did she provide you with a direct number?"

"No," I said, giving Quan a glare. "I don't have a direct number to the goddess of death and destruction." I glanced down at my mark. "What she did to me was a curse, not a blessing. We're not friends, and I don't worship her. She's not *my* goddess."

"No?" Quan asked. "You don't think she knows you've been poisoned? After all, you are *her* Marked One. Has she offered to help you?"

"No, she hasn't."

"Perhaps, if you ask nicely, she will make a special appearance just for you and fix everything?" Quan suggested. "Does that sound like the Kali you know?"

I thought back to all of my interactions with the dark goddess of death and destruction. She was more likely to appear and accelerate my poisoning, claiming it would be an excellent teaching moment or the perfect way to impact my personal growth, helping me to embrace my inner *Aspis* by stepping over to the dark side.

I shuddered reflexively.

"Not really, no," I said. "She's more likely to push me further into the whole 'dark immortal thing' somehow. That seems more like her style."

Quan nodded.

"I wouldn't count on her—or *any* god's—help," she said. "They prefer to watch and see what happens before taking action. Then, when they do act, it's usually to *their* benefit, not yours."

Hades' words came back to me: *You could opt to let the poisoning run its course. I don't know what the outcome will be, but knowing you, I'm certain it will be interesting.*

He probably omitted the second half of that statement, where the outcome would be interesting for all of ten seconds, right before I was blasted to dark immortal atoms to preserve the "balance".

"The lost elder rune is a forbidden rune to your sect," Aria said, interrupting my thoughts and looking at Monty.

"Will you run the risk of erasure from Verity, knowing the consequences?"

"Verity has made their intentions known," Monty said. "I believe my erasure is currently at the top of their list. Yes, I will run the risk."

"Can you successfully perform a nexus purifier?" Aria asked, turning to Quan. "*Without* sacrificing the target?"

"Yes," Quan said, looking off to the side. She was probably thinking of Lyn, whom she had failed to save. "I can and have."

"Very well," Aria said. "I refuse to allow another dark immortal to enter this plane unchallenged. One way or another, we will prevent Simon from transforming into one. Quan, the Crucible's chamber will be made available to you and Simon."

"Thank you," Quan said with a short bow. "I will get him ready."

"Do you remember where it is?" Aria asked. "Or do you need an escort?"

"I recall its location, thank you."

Aria gave Quan a long look. For a moment, I thought the wordweaver was going to eject her from the property, then she smiled.

"Of course you do," Aria said, her voice soft, but with an undertone of steel. "I will provide an escort regardless. I can't have you getting lost in our corridors."

Quan paused for a second, then bowed.

"As you wish," she said. "Thank you for the use of the Crucible."

"It will remain in stasis throughout your use, but we are on a limited timetable," Aria said. "Tana will move against us soon."

"How many other dark immortals have there been besides Kana?" I asked, concerned at the finality of her statement.

Somehow, I knew if we failed, she wouldn't. There was no way she was going to allow me to live to be a dark immortal. "Are there any still around that we can consult?"

"None currently living on this plane," Aria said, her expression dark. She looked at Quan. "Begin the blood lessons immediately. He must be able to initiate the storm-blood within a day's time. Verity will not remain idle. They *will* mount an attack, and we must be ready."

"But they don't have jurisdiction on wordweaver lands," I said. "They would violate that?"

"Faced with what they consider a dark mage"—she glanced at Monty—"and a potential dark immortal who is bonded to a hellhound?" Aria replied. "For that, the High Tribunal would violate everything. Verity will attack in the next few days. They only need the Tribunal's approval and Cain will make sure they get it. I suggest you make your preparations."

"I am not a dark mage," Monty said, firmly, "and never will be."

"You used a lost elder *blood* rune," Aria said. "In Verity's eyes, the use of the rune along with your association with Simon puts you squarely in dark mage territory."

"They are fools."

"Powerful ones at that," Aria said. "Their view of the world and magic is monochromatic. Do not mistake the narrowness of their vision for weakness. The position they hold gives them a singularity of purpose that is difficult to sway. It is one they utilize to keep an iron grip of power over many. You would do well to keep that in mind when you try to wrest Ines from their grasp."

"I shall," Monty said. "I only need to open her eyes to their true motives."

"Someone needs to stop Verity," I said. "They sound just like bullies."

"That is a battle for another day," Aria said. "Today we focus on getting ready for the battle that approaches. I will prepare the inner courtyard to perform the Rule of Three casts. It rests over one of the major ley-lines, and is a central place of power."

"That sounds dangerous," I asked. "The last place of power I was on nearly got me killed."

"Places of power must be treated with the respect they deserve," she said, looking at me. "Our place of power makes the energy flowing through Scola Tower appear insignificant in comparison. It will be enough to do what must be done."

"That's not ominous or anything," I said, under my breath. "How did you know about Scola Tower?"

"Your activity there has gained you attention," she said. "Some of it unwanted, I'm sure."

Aria unfolded her legs and stood gracefully—a move that would've had me toppling head first into the pool if I had tried to do the same.. She began walking out of the courtyard.

"Thank you," I said, even though she had just promised to eliminate me from existence if we failed. "Thank you for trying this option."

She paused in her steps without turning.

"Before we are done, you will curse our names many times over," she said. "I hope you are ready. The blood required to perform the Rule of Three in this cast will be provided by the immortal among us."

Oh, shit.

TWENTY

"How much blood is that?" I asked when Aria had gone. "Do I even have that much blood?"

"It is a substantial amount, but you should be in no danger of total exsanguination," Monty assured me as he looked off to the side, as if remembering something. "I'm going to need to prepare some items. I will be back shortly. Quan, please begin the blood lessons without me."

Monty headed out of the courtyard.

That left me alone with Quan.

"I really need to go see my hellhound before we start these bloody lessons," I said and made to leave the courtyard. "I'll be back in a—"

"No," Quan said, blocking my path. "We start your lessons now. Please sit."

"What? Here? Now?"

"Yes," she said. "Your hellhound will find you if he needs you. Right now, he is being served very large bowls of meat. I doubt he will be searching for you anytime soon."

I checked through my bond to Peaches and felt a sense of

contentment. He had probably inhaled several bowls by now, the black hole.

"I hope you have a plan B, because I have never initiated anything like a stormblood in my life," I said, sitting on the low stool again and remembering the devastation Josephine had unleashed with her stormblood. "Now you want me to learn how to start one in one day? I'd say that's highly optimistic. My magic missile nearly killed me last night."

"You already know how to do this," Quan said, sitting on a bench opposite mine. "Call forth your weapon."

"*That* would be a bad idea," I said warily. "My magic missile nearly sliced through...everything. Ebonsoul would be worse. It's a necromantic siphon with a dash of seraph now. If I can't control it, that would be bad for both of us."

"*Form* your weapon," she said again. It wasn't a request. "I will deal with any imminent attacks."

I looked at her in disbelief and shook my head.

"This is a bad idea," I said again. "I don't want to hurt you."

"You can't," she said, extending an arm around. "Not here, in this place. Form your weapon, *please*."

"Don't say I didn't warn you," I said, closing my eyes and feeling for the sensation of Ebonsoul inside of me. "If I were you, I would wait on the other side of the courtyard."

"Your concern is appreciated but unfounded," she replied. "I'm safe right here."

After a few more seconds or searching, I felt it.

The cold punched into my chest.

I opened my eyes and saw my breath escape my lips. The cold raced through me, plunging my body into arctic temperatures. It was colder than I had ever felt.

"Co...cold," I stammered as my body shivered. "Never... never felt like this before."

"Control it," Quan said, her voice steady. "Materialize the weapon."

I focused on the cold and felt it wrap itself around my body. I mentally pushed it down and away, to my arm, and then to my hand.

A silver mist had formed around my arm. It slowly snaked its way down my arm and hovered around my hand. I focused harder, fighting against the bitter cold.

"Why is it so cold?" I asked, focusing on my hand. "It's never been like this."

"The sensation of cold is a result of your internal disarray," she said. "You must bring the energy into harmony with your new state. Now focus."

"Working on it," I said, willing the energy into form. "It's not as easy as I make it look."

The silver mist shifted suddenly, changing colors. It whirled in my hand as shades of violet, black, and gold shot through the silver. A few moments later, I held a pulsing Ebonsoul in my hand.

There was no way I could anticipate the icepick of pain stabbing in the back of my head. I yelled out and grabbed my neck. Quan began gesturing as the pain squeezed my temples.

It felt like my head was caught in a vise.

"You must get control, Simon," Quan said. "You have to control the weapon. You can do it. Breathe."

I held on to the sound of her voice like a drowning man latches on to a life line in the ocean. I anchored my mind to her voice and slowly grabbed hold of the power racing in and around me.

"That's it," she said calmly. "You can do it. Take control of the energy. See the energy. Make it a rope; each facet is a strand. Tie them together. Join them."

I mentally saw the three strands of energy, one black, one

violet, and one gold. I joined them together in my mind, braiding them into one rope of combined energy.

Ebonsoul pulsed in my hand as the energy coursed through me. I looked down at the blade and saw the runes fluctuate with color. Snatches of information were bombarding my mind: symbols I didn't recognize, runes and intricate designs embedded in circles.

"It's too much information," I said, gasping for breath. "I don't understand any of it."

"Yet," Quan said. "Whatever Orethe placed in your weapon, you're not strong enough to decipher it yet. You need to create a space in your mind. Think of it as a storage room. Let all that information go into the storage space."

"What...what happens if I can't put it in this storage room?"

"You will go mad—eventually," she said. "Your brain can only handle so much sensory input. At some point, it will shortcircuit. Now, focus, and I will assist you."

She whispered some words I could barely understand, but the meaning behind the words was clear. She was amplifying my energy somehow.

"You can't amplify this," I said through clenched teeth. "It's too much."

A look of surprise crossed her face.

"The fact that you could understand some of what I'm saying lets me know we are progressing along the right path," she said. "Now shut down the information from the blade."

I imagined myself shoving all the images, sounds, and information into the back of my mind. I opened a large vault door and pushed it all in. Then I closed that door, locking it with a loud *slam*.

My mind suddenly became quiet and still.

"I did it," I said, surprised. "I can hear myself think."

"You did," she said, wiping the sweat from her brow. "Now, we can begin."

"Begin?" I asked, incredulous as Ebonsoul vanished. "What do you mean? I just stored all the information away."

"That wasn't a blood lesson," she said. "That was getting your mind still enough to *begin* the blood lessons. Now we can start the first. Are you ready?"

"How many lessons are there?" I asked, trying not to sound as exhausted as I felt. "Edith said there was only one."

"I'm not Edith," Quan said with an edge. "Do not compare me to her."

"I wasn't comparing, I just... How many lessons are there?"

"Three," she said, her expression unreadable. "The foundation, the structure, and the execution. All three will be excruciating, the execution worst of all."

"Of course they are," I said, resigned to the pain. "Why would I think blood lessons would be painless? It's right there in the name, isn't it?"

"Life *is* pain, Marked One," Quan said, getting to her feet. "Anyone who says different is selling something."

"Are we going somewhere?"

"Yes," she said, leaving the courtyard. "Follow me. The Crucible awaits."

TWENTY-ONE

We descended several levels to the interior of the Cloisters. I noticed that, as we walked the corridors, she didn't get lost.

"How are you not getting lost in here?" I asked. "These corridors are designed to form a maze."

"I'm not using my eyes," she said. "Over here. This is the space that will serve our needs."

She pointed to a featureless section of the stone wall.

"Are you sure?" I asked, confused. "That just looks like the—"

She pushed on the wall, and a thin door opened.

"This is the Crucible."

We had stepped into a large featureless room. It was empty except for a plain small, plain stone basin in the center of the floor. The walls, floor, and ceiling were made of the same pink marble that was used all over the Cloisters.

Each of the surfaces was covered with softly glowing violet runes. I was able to decipher some of the runes, but the symbols were out of context. It was similar to understanding one word in a long sentence made up of foreign words. They made no sense.

"What is this place?" I asked, looking around. "Are we still in the Cloisters?"

She looked at me as if I had suffered a brain injury.

"Where do you think you are?" she asked. "Of course we are still in the Cloisters. Where else would we be?"

"I'm just asking," I said, holding up a hand. "No need to bite my head off."

"This space is several levels above the inner courtyard," she said, glancing at the floor, "where we will perform the casts. As such, it rests on a ley-line, but is not a place of power."

"It's a training space," I said, recognizing the familiar feel of a space designed to impart knowledge...and pain. "Do the wordweavers train in here?"

"Not specifically in this space, no," she said. "This room was provided for us to accelerate your training. Think of it as a laboratory of sorts."

"A lab? Really?" I said, looking around again. "I'm honored."

"You should be," Quan replied, following my gaze. "Aria rarely allows non-wordweavers to use the Crucible."

"The Crucible?" I asked. "Why does that sound unpleasant?"

"Because it is...for you."

I looked at the space again.

The basin in the center of the room was filled with a dark liquid. I stepped close to the edge of the basin, taking a look at it.

"Is that...blood?"

Quan looked down at the liquid, and then at me. She shook her head slowly.

"No. That...is you," she said, pointing at the stone basin. "It is an indicator of your current state. Dark, murky, unclear. It is the present state of your mind, your body, and your spirit." She shook her head in disapproval as she looked at the liquid. "You are a mess."

I looked down at the liquid in the basin one more time before stepping back. While I agreed with her assessment, there was no need to be insulting about it.

"The insults are unnecessary," I said. "You do realize I'm currently poisoned? A little messiness is expected, given the current state of affairs."

"Excuse me while I shed a tear for your current situation," she said, staring at me. "Are you going to remind me now how you are not a mage...again?"

"I'm not," I said. "Yet everyone expects me to—"

"Enough," she said, slashing a hand through the air. "Enough with the self-pity. Do you expect Tristan to come and rescue you every time you get yourself into some life-and-death situation?"

Now I was getting mad.

"That is not true," I shot back. "We work as a team."

"A team? Really?" she scoffed. "What part do you play? Designated victim?"

"You don't know what you're talking about," I said, anger lacing my words. "I was the one who stopped the disintegrator last night. Do you know how many times I've stuck my neck out into danger when Monty was facing some insane creature?"

"Does quivering in a corner count as sticking your neck out?"

"Quivering...*quivering* in a corner?" I asked, raising my voice. "Do you know who I am? What I've gone through? The beings I've faced?"

"Do you?" she asked, gently. "Do you recall what you've gone through to get here? The enemies seeking your destruction?"

My anger evaporated.

"I do," I said, letting out a long breath. "Thanks."

"Sometimes, when things are looking bleak, we forget who we really are," she said. "Your enemies are counting on fear ruling your mind. Once it does, your access to your power is diminished, if not gone entirely. Every so often, it is good to remind yourself who you really are. Who are you?"

"I am Simon Strong, Marked of Kali, bondmate to Peaches the hellhound, bond brother and Aspis to Mage Tristan Montague," I said. "I am the bearer of Ebonsoul, siphon, seraph, and necromantic weapon."

She nodded.

"Who are you to your enemies?"

"I am the fear of their darkest thoughts, the nightmare that never ends. I am relentless, unstoppable and inevitable. I am death."

She raised an eyebrow at me and cocked her head to one side.

"Okay, whoa—dial it back a bit there, Dark Knight," Quan said. "How many cups of coffee did you have today?"

"Sorry," I said, rubbing my neck. "I got a little carried away there."

"No kidding," she said, giving me a look. "But...the next time someone says you're not a mage, don't take it personally, because what you are can be so much more than 'just' a mage."

"Understood," I said, sheepishly. "I was laying it on there a little thick, wasn't I?"

"Slathering even," she said and composed herself. "Let's get started. Do you remember the Rule of Three?"

"Catalyst, cleansing, and containment," I said. "Is the foundation the catalyst? Are they related?"

"Yes. Right now, this space, the Crucible, is the foundation," she said, extending an arm around the room. "Before you can see the structure, you must understand the foundation."

"Right, the foundation," I said, still taking in the room. I noticed, with some concern that the door had disappeared. "The foundation of what, exactly?"

She raised a hand and the designs on her face began to glow a soft blue.

"These lessons weren't always called the blood lessons," she said, looking at her hand. "Long ago, they were taught with books in a formal class setting—until my father, Master Li Toh, changed the process of teaching."

Somehow, I had a feeling I wasn't going to like the change in process.

"He felt," she continued, "that the lessons were not effective enough. Some information was being lost in transmission. So, when the time came for me to learn my first lessons as a mage, he transformed the method of transmission."

"He used you as a guinea pig for his new method?" I asked, focused on the glowing designs on her face. "What was the method called before they were called blood lessons?"

"Irrelevant, at least according to him," she said. "He felt that if he could impart the knowledge directly into the blood of his students, they would excel. They would retain the information he wanted to share and build upon it."

"That...sounds painful," I said. "Did it work?"

"It was brutally efficient, with only one downside."

"It was a bloody mess?"

She gave me a look that warned me the ice I was standing on was currently over shark-infested waters, and it was cracking. I decided to tone down the humor.

"The attrition rate was unacceptable to the elders of the White Phoenix," she said. "Turns out the blood lessons were killing more mages than teaching them."

"Sounds like it was time for a change," I said. "Something a little less lethal."

"He did," she said. "He adapted and modified the process, resulting in more mages learning and surviving."

"That process—let's do *that* process," I said. "I'm all in."

"For a select few though, his children included, he kept the old method," she continued, making a fist. "The blood lessons. He wanted us to be stronger, to excel, and to be able to withstand any attack. The White Phoenix never allowed the blood lessons to be used again."

"I know this may seem obvious, but why are they called blood lessons?"

"Two reasons," she said, holding up two fingers. "Blood, at its most fundamental nature, is based on the Rule of Three."

"I'm not following," I said. "Blood is blood."

"No, wrong," she corrected. "Blood is based on three cells. Red blood cells carry oxygen to the parts of the body. They are the catalysts for energy—for life. White blood cells fight infection, they cleanse the body. Platelets clot the blood, containing any damage. Catalyst, cleansing, containment. The Rule of Three. The plasma they all exist in, is the reality in which the Rule of Three operates. The context is decisive."

"That is...I've never thought about it like that," I said, taken by surprise at her simple yet complex explanation. "What's the second reason?"

"That, I will share with you shortly."

"Why are you making a fist?" I asked. "You never did answer my question—what foundation am I supposed to understand?"

"Everything starts with the foundation," she said, looking at me now. "Draw your weapon again—if you can."

"You're not serious," I said. "If I cut you with Ebonsoul... Well, actually I don't know what will happen if I cut you with Ebonsoul now that it's a necromantic weapon, but I don't want to find out, and I'm sure you don't want to find out either."

"Simon, if Verity gets their hands on you, it won't matter that you are cursed alive," she said. "Being immortal doesn't mean you can't die."

"Actually, that's exactly what it's supposed to mean," I protested. "It's right there in the word—exempt from death."

"Verity knows how to kill immortals," she said, stepping into a defensive stance. "They will kill you, but first they will kill everyone you know. When you beg them for death, they will refuse, and then, near the end, when you cling to life, when a spark of hope flares within you, they will snatch it from you."

"How do you know this?"

"What is the foundation, Simon?"

I looked at her, perplexed.

"How should I know?" I said. "We haven't discussed the foundation of anything."

"What is the foundation, Simon?"

"You just asked me that," I said, raising my voice. "My answer is still the same. I don't know."

"What is the foundation?"

"I. Don't. Know."

"Then you must learn," she said with a slight nod. "Allow me the honor of sharing my wisdom with you."

I should have known what those words meant. I had had enough lessons with Master Yat that I should've expected what came next. Instead, I missed all the signs of my impending pain.

"Finally," I said with a sigh. "What is the foundation?"

She slid forward and attacked.

TWENTY-TWO

The first strike felt like someone hit me across the chest with a twenty-pound sledgehammer. The blow sent me flying, bouncing me off the not-so-soft granite wall behind me with a *thud*.

"You're too slow," she said, closing the distance. "What's the foundation?"

"I don't know."

"Wrong answer," she said, driving an elbow into my ribs. "Were you not paying attention? You *know* the answer. Once you understand, the Crucible is designed to assist you—but first, you must understand."

The elbow strike shoved me to the side with force, as my ribs screamed in protest. I pushed off the wall and into a backhand across the face, rotating me clockwise as I stumbled back to the wall.

Memories of my meetings with Karma flashed in my mind as my jaw threatened to leave my body. The coppery taste of blood filled my mouth as I spit a generous amount on the floor.

"I'd understand faster without getting pounded into paste," I said. "I don't know the foundation!"

"Maybe not, but now you know the second reason," she said, shaking her head suddenly as if catching the whiff of some stench. A moment later she had composed herself again. "What is the foundation?"

I moved back and entered a defensive stance. There was no way I could form Ebonsoul while I was doing my best punching-bag impression.

Even if I could form my blade, she would strip it from me before I had a chance to use it against her. I had no illusions about her fighting skill; I had seen her in action. I was outclassed and outmatched.

If this kept up, I was dead.

My only chance was to answer the question before she beat me unconscious. My mind raced—she said I *knew* the answer.

The attacks were a result of my giving incorrect responses to her question: *What is the foundation?*

Context was decisive.

She had to be referring to foundations in a magical context. What was the foundation of magic?

Knowledge. It had to be knowledge.

"Knowledge," I said, confidently. "It's knowledge."

She disappeared from my view and reappeared next to me.

"Wrong," she said, driving a knee into my midsection, doubling me over. The knee was followed by a hammerfist to the back of my head, which drove me to the ground. Once I was on the floor, she graced the side of my head with a kick designed to punt me into next week. "What is the foundation?"

The room tilted in several directions at once as I lay on the cool marble floor, not daring to move.

"I just want to go on the record," I said, weakly lifting an arm. "Your blood lessons suck."

"Is that your answer?"

"No! No," I said, quickly. "Give me a second."

"One," she said, and waved an arm in my direction. A wave of energy raced across the floor, lifting me up and tossing me hard across the room. I slid on the marble floor and came to a sudden stop at the stone basin with a hard *crunch*. "What's the foundation?"

The basin didn't so much as budge as my body impacted the side. If we kept this up, she was going to break me into small bits.

My body was flushed with heat as my curse fought to keep me conscious. My muscles spasmed from the pounding Quan was sharing with me, shaking against their will as I got to all fours.

The vibration in my body was making it impossible to concentrate.

The vibrations.

Frequency.

Something shifted in my mind. A memory, a thought. A forgotten conversation with Monty. A thwacking by Yat as he shared a lesson. Some part of my mind wondered if Yat had a hand in designing these blood lessons.

Everything vibrated at a specific frequency.

That was the foundation.

That is what I needed to do. She had given me the instructions: *The Crucible is designed to assist you, but first, you must understand.*

I needed to align to the frequency of the room.

I took a deep breath as she approached. Calming my mind, I removed everything that wasn't frequency. I felt the vibration of the energy in the room and aligned to it.

The runes in the room flared for a few seconds and I felt a

surge of power in my body. Quan had closed the distance and drove a fist into the ground.

I pushed off the basin, sliding away and narrowly avoiding the blow. I rolled to my feet, feeling revitalized as Quan appeared in front of me. She unleashed a barrage of attacks. Much to my surprise, I managed to parry or avoid all of them.

She stepped back and raised an eyebrow at me before putting a fist in her palm and giving me a short bow.

"What is the foundation, Simon?"

"Frequency," I said, returning the bow. "Everything vibrates at a specific frequency."

"Correct," she said, stepping over to the basin and motioning for me to join her. "Look."

I stepped over warily, ready for any surprise attacks.

The liquid in the basin had become lighter. The inky blackness was gone. Now, it was just plain dirty looking. I was still a mess, just less of one at the moment.

"Study this feeling," she said, extending an arm around the room. "Feel it and absorb it. This is the first step in initiating the stormblood. You must align to its frequency before you begin."

I closed my eyes and let the feeling of the Crucible wash over me. I wouldn't forget this feeling. The aches and pains in my body would make sure of that, at least until my curse dealt with them.

"I feel it," I said.

"Good," she said. "Let's continue."

TWENTY-THREE

She placed her hand in the basin.

The liquid whirled around her hand before settling again. The room had shifted from pink marble to white marble with gold undertones.

Circles and diagrams were on every wall, with lines of runic symbols going from one circle to another.

In some areas, symbols were connected by lines and runes, intersecting each other and joining several other circles on different walls.

This was repeated on every surface I could see.

"The second lesson," Quan said, materializing a short, silver rune-covered blade attached to a long chain and a metal circle. "Once again, the Crucible will assist you, after you understand."

"A *kyoketsu-shoge*," I said, looking at her weapon. "That looks dangerous."

"It's no siphon," she said, glancing at her weapon, "but I hear getting stabbed or slashed is painful no matter what blade is used. Form your weapon."

I reached inward for Ebonsoul and the silver-black mist formed around my arm instantly. There was no cold and no pain. With another thought, my blade materialized in my hand.

"That was...easier?" I said, looking down at Ebonsoul. "Why was it easier this time?"

"Once you answer my question, you'll know the reason," Quan said.

"Your blade may not be a siphon, but this one is," I warned. "I don't think this is a good idea. If I cut you—"

"Is it?"

"Is it what?"

"A siphon," she said, pointing at Ebonsoul. "Look again."

I looked down at Ebonsoul and noticed that all of the runes along the length of the blade were dormant. It looked like an ordinary, insanely sharp and scary short sword.

"What happened?"

She let out a length of chain. The tip of the blade touched the marble floor before she pulled it short and started twirling the knife next to her in a large circle.

"What is the structure, Simon?"

I didn't waste energy denying that I knew the answer. Somewhere in the recesses of my brain I had the answer. I just had to survive long enough to find it.

Remembering the lesson from the previous room, I expanded my senses and felt for Quan's frequency. In less than a second, I felt it and aligned myself to her. She nodded in approval.

It wasn't a second too soon, as her blade shot forward in a straight thrust. I managed to parry the attack and slide to the side with no margin for error.

She retracted the blade, ducking forward as the chain sailed overhead. The blade wrapped itself around her body without cutting her as she straightened up, rotating and adding momentum to her weapon.

In a split second, she released the blade again. I sensed the attack half a second before she unleashed it. I moved back, out of range. I didn't realize that, in her rotation, she had given the chain slack.

What I thought was out of range turned out to be the perfect range. I parried the attack right into my opposite shoulder. I bit back a scream as she yanked the blade out of my skin.

Blood flowed freely from my wound.

"What is the structure?" she said, as the chain started up again. She paused for a moment, looking at the blood. Then she shook her head and refocused on me. "The answer is all around you."

I waited for a few seconds until my curse stopped the blood flow. If this turned out to be a prolonged lesson, I would bleed out before I got the answer.

I stole a glance at the walls around me. There was no way I was going to be able to read all those symbols before she shish-kebabbed me with her blade.

"I don't understand all these symbols," I said, ducking under her blade and rolling to the side as she pulled it back. She almost wrapped it around my neck and I made a mental note to be aware of her retractions. "I'm still on basic runes 101."

She twirled the chain again, and then did something unexpected—she dashed forward with the blade in her hand, closing the distance between us.

"What the—?" I said, trying to backpedal. She caught me flatfooted since I was expecting long-range attacks. It never occurred to me that she would engage in close-quarters combat. "Shit."

I parried the first thrust and ducked under another slash. I slashed upward at her wrist, which she pulled back, letting her knife fall over my shoulder and catching it under my arm.

I thrust forward, but she twisted her body to the side, avoiding my attack, before wrapping the chain around my arm. She pulled down, attempting to stab me, but I used my opposite hand to divert the pull.

She grabbed more chain and tried to tangle up my free arm, while slashing with the blade. I reversed my grip on Ebonsoul and brought it down in front of me.

She pulled both hands back, using one to push my chest and throw off my attack while the other caught the extra chain. She lunged forward to wrap the chain around my neck in a loose noose.

I ducked under the chain and slashed at her midsection. She rotated away from my slash, ending up with her back facing me. Before I could react, she bent at the waist and pulled hard on the chain she still held—the chain that was still wrapped around one of my shoulders.

I flew over her waist and landed on the marble floor hard, the wind punched out of my lungs. Stars danced in my vision as she brought her blade down.

I rolled to the side and barely avoided her last attack.

I was gasping for air and she just stood there, looking at me calmly as if we were having a relaxing conversation.

"What is the structure?" she asked with a slight smile. "I gave you the answer only moments ago."

"Repeatedly trying to perforate me doesn't sound like the right answer," I said between gasps. "I don't know."

"Wrong answer," she said and threw her blade.

It went wide and I thought she had missed. I should have known better. She tugged at the chain in a sideways whip-cracking motion, causing the blade to travel horizontally and bury itself in my thigh.

I fell to one knee with a groan as blood poured down my leg. That's when it hit me: I had her weapon. Yes, it was buried in my leg, but if it was buried in my leg, she couldn't throw it at me.

While we remained connected, I had the advantage. I gripped the chain slick with my blood and held on before she could tug the blade out.

We were connected.

Shit. That was the structure.

Everything is connected.

I looked around the Crucible. The answer had been right in front of me the whole time. Every symbol, every set of runes, every circle, was connected to one another.

Nothing stood on its own. The entire room was one connected entity. I shook my head as the realization hit me.

"Everything is connected," I said, pulling out her blade. "It's all connected."

She retracted the blade.

It disappeared before it reached her hand. She walked over to the basin and pointed. I limped over to where she stood. The liquid inside the stone basin was clean enough to see the bottom, but it was still cloudy.

"That," she said, looking down at the basin, "was the correct answer. Look around. Everything is connected. This room, our fight, your bonds, the energy you possess within. It's all connected. The stormblood you will initiate, not only connects you to Tristan, but it connects you to each of us. Remember this. Learn this."

I nodded and limped over to the nearest wall.

"Can we take a time out?" I asked. "Not that I'm not grateful for the blood lessons, but maybe we can take a break? Pick this up later or tomorrow?"

She gave me a smile and nodded.

I don't understand how I kept missing the red flags of

pain. I blame the repeated beatings and the poison coursing through my body for clouding my reason. She came over to where I stood, leaning against the wall, facing me.

"I understand," she said, her voice calm and gentle. "You want to take a break?"

"I would really appreciate a break, yes."

She moved so fast I thought I imagined it. It wasn't until I felt the pain shoot up my arm when I realized she had broken my forearm with a downward knife hand strike.

"Once your arm heals," she said, heading to the stone basin again. "Break over."

A string of curses raced through my brain. I made certain none of them escaped my lips.

"That," I said, wiping the thin sheen of sweat on my brow as my curse knitted my arm, "was not the kind of break I meant."

She turned to face me, her expression fierce.

"Do you think this is a game?" she asked. "There are people out there who want you dead. Who want Tristan... dead. Your hellhound...dead. Me...dead. They want to wipe the wordweavers off the map just for lending us assistance, and you want to take a break?"

I remained silent.

I knew better than to try and answer her. She was right. If I didn't get this poison under control, my days were numbered. Tana, Ines, Edith, and the rest of Verity would come to eliminate all of us.

"I'm sorry," I said after a few seconds. "I wasn't thinking."

"Do not lie to me, Simon," she said. "More importantly, don't lie to yourself. You *were* thinking...selfishly. You were only thinking of *your* pain and discomfort. The world is much larger than just you. The sooner you learn that, the better."

"You're right," I said, stepping off the wall with a wince. "I'm ready for the next lesson."

"No. You aren't."
She plunged her arm into the basin.

TWENTY-FOUR

The liquid whirled around her arm again.

When it stilled, we stood in the Crucible, but this time the runes on the walls, floor, and ceiling were black on bright white marble. They pulsed slowly, the surge of power present all around me.

The runes were different this time.

Each wall held one large symbol that filled the surface it was on.

Every rune was the same.

"What does it mean?" I said, looking at the vaguely familiar symbol. "Do you know?"

"Please sit," Quan said, sitting in *seiza* on one side of the basin. She motioned for me to sit opposite her on the other side of the basin. "This is the third and final blood lesson."

I sat down on my knees warily, expecting her to launch the basin at me or something. Somehow, having a conversation seemed counter to my recent experience with the violence of the blood lessons.

"You're not going to attack me?" I asked, staring at her and tensing my body. "Is this some kind of trick?"

She raised a hand and I almost flinched in response.

The liquid in the basin formed into an orb, similar to the one Aria had created with the energy from my magic missile. It hovered over the basin, slowly rotating in place.

Even though the liquid was cloudy when it was in the basin, in orb form, it fluctuated between gold, violet, and black. I noticed the black area was fully half of the orb and slowly filling in the gold and violet areas.

"This is your final blood lesson," she said. "The black is the poison currently in your system. The gold represents the necromancy recently imparted to you by Orethe, and the violet is your core energy—what makes you...you."

"What do I need to do?" I asked, my gaze fixed on the orb in front of me. "Can I remove the poison?"

"What is the execution?" she asked, starting the lesson. "Remember: the Crucible holds the answer."

"Can I ask other questions?" I asked. "Without getting whacked?"

"You may ask three questions pertaining to the lesson."

If the Crucible held the answer like the last two times, it seemed that the first question would be to know the meaning of the runes around me.

"What does the rune mean?" I asked, looking at the pulsing runes around me. "The true definition, please."

She nodded in approval.

"The rune inscribed around us means mutable."

Mutable, which meant capable of change. The context was the execution. I was wandering into mage theory territory, and my brain was starting to hurt.

I looked at the orb and focused on the black area. If the black area symbolized the poison, it would be important to know if I could remove it.

I remembered her words regarding removing the poison:

The only person who can do that is the person who put it there in the first place. Who poisoned you?

"Can the poison be removed by anyone?"

"No one can remove the poison in your body at this point," she said. "It has progressed too far."

The last question would be the most important. Everything hinged on this.

"Can I change the poison inside me?"

She gave me a tight smile and a nod, gazing at the orb in front of us.

"Those were excellent questions," she said. "Yes, *you* can change the poison within you."

"What is the execution?" I said, mostly to myself. "The execution. I have another question, one not related to the lesson."

"Ask," she said. "I will not answer if it in anyway pertains to the lesson. Do you understand?"

I nodded.

"Judging from how this lesson is set up," I started, "I understand you can't help me complete the lesson. Why are you here?"

She gestured and formed a sheathed black-and-red sword, resting it next to her. Even from where I sat, I could tell it possessed a powerful energy signature.

A familiar energy signature.

"Do you recall the first time we met?" she asked. "I was in pursuit of the Phoenix Tail, the item Davros stole from my sect."

"I remember."

"This," she said, tapping the sword next to her, "is the Phoenix Blade. An artifact of the White Phoenix. It possesses a particular quality—aside from being immensely powerful, which I'm certain you can sense. It has one special purpose: it was created to kill gods."

A *kamikira*.

"A god-killer," I said, nodding. It was all starting to make sense. "That's why you're still here. You're the final check and balance if I don't pass this lesson."

She nodded her head slowly, still gazing at the orb that signified my power.

"If you fail to arrest the poison in your system, beginning your transformation into a dark immortal, I am to make sure you never leave the Crucible."

It made sense.

Now I understood why Monty wasn't a part of my blood lessons. He knew that the last lesson would require he be willing to take my life.

"Monty knew," I said. "He knew what the last blood lesson was, didn't he?"

"Yes," she said. "He requested you be spared this last lesson if you passed the earlier two."

"I'm going to guess the answer was no?"

"There are no exceptions to the blood lessons," Quan said, her voice firm. "It has always been and will always be three. They are always different and always the same."

"That's not cryptic at all."

"Please begin."

I refocused on the orb in front of me.

The answers to my questions involved change: the poison couldn't be removed, but it could be changed. This all sounded so familiar. I couldn't remove it, but I could change it? How? I wasn't a mage. I had the potential to be so much more. How could I change this poison inside of me?

In the back of my mind, then, I saw the problem. The solution arrived a few seconds later, gave me a *what are you waiting for?* glare and crossed its arms, tapping its foot in impatience.

The solution was simple and brutal. It really drove home why these lessons were called blood lessons.

I formed Ebonsoul.

All of the runes along its length were blazing with power. Ebonsoul was fully powered this time.

"Do you have your answer?" Quan asked, resting a hand on the Phoenix Blade. "What is the execution?"

"Energy can neither be created nor destroyed," I said. "Only converted from one form to another. The first Law of Thermodynamics."

"Correct," she said. "How will you change this poison?"

"At first, I thought I had to do something to this orb," I said, pointing at the orb floating in front of us. "Then I realized that this orb is only a representation of what is happening inside of me. This orb is for you, to monitor me, in case you need to end me."

"Again, correct," she said. "It serves the same purpose as the basin."

"So, not being a mage..."

She raised an eyebrow.

"But having the potential to be so much more," I added quickly, "I realized that the solution is in the blood lessons. You said it yourself: they are always the same and they are always different. No two people go through identical blood lessons, but they all go through identical blood lessons in terms of their severity."

"You have been spending much time around mages," she said. "It seems you have been paying attention."

"The answer, then."

I lifted Ebonsoul into my hands, positioning it in front of my belly.

"I have to use Ebonsoul to transform the poison and restore the balance," I said, my voice grim. "The siphoning properties of my blade will transform the energy, which can't be destroyed, but can be converted into something that won't turn me into a dark immortal."

Quan removed the Phoenix Blade from its sheath and rose to one knee, holding the blade over her head.

It was my turn to raise an eyebrow.

"Your theory is sound," she said, "but I must take every precaution. Whenever you are ready."

"If this doesn't work," I said. "Tell Monty I was honored to fight by his side."

"I will," she said. "Your hellhound will be returned to Hades safe and sound. You have my word. Anyone else?"

I nodded.

"Chi," I said. "We never did get to fix things between us. I...It's too late now."

"Yes, it is," she said. "What words would you have me give her?"

"Tell her she always had my heart."

"I will."

"Thank you."

I took a deep breath and let it out slowly. I looked down at Ebonsoul for a second and then looked up at Quan. Her eyes were resolute as we locked gazes. She gave me a small nod and I plunged Ebonsoul into my abdomen.

It was when her eyes went vacant that I realized something was wrong.

TWENTY-FIVE

My world exploded in a surge of power and energy.

The pain and agony followed shortly after.

Ebonsoul—a siphon—was designed to take power and infuse it into me. By stabbing myself, I had created an energy loop. It was draining and filling me simultaneously.

My world suddenly ground to a halt; the heady smell of lotus blossoms and earth after a hard rain filled my lungs. This was followed by the sharp smell of cut oranges and an aroma hinting of cinnamon permeating the air.

I knew for a fact that I hadn't pressed my mark.

I looked down at my hands just to double check. My mark was untouched—covered in large amounts of blood—but untouched.

"Hello, Splinter."

"Karma," I managed around the agony. "Nice of you to drop in. Maybe we can talk later? I'm a little busy right now."

She stepped into view looking breathtaking.

She was wearing a Dior sleeveless form-fitting black gown. On her feet she wore a variation of Vietri's Moon Star shoes in black with red accents. There was a small fortune alone between the dress and shoes.

On one shoulder, I could see a deep red letter B tattoo, done in deep red.

Her hair was pulled back in a tight ponytail with red lace intertwined throughout its length. I didn't see the several small sharp-looking knives as accessories that she usually used, but she wore two black, long, diamond studded hairpins which looked as deadly as they were fashionable.

"Am I overdressed for the funeral?" she said, looking down at her outfit. "This is special occasion after all. It's not every day an immortal dies."

"If you don't mind," I said with a groan, trying to keep my intestines where they belonged, "I'm trying *not* to die here."

"That does look painful," Karma said as she stepped closer and crouched down. "Are you practicing seppuku?" She turned to look at Quan. "Is this your second? She looks determined to give you a permanent haircut."

"She's only there to make sure...make sure I don't turn into a dark immortal," I said around the pain in my stomach. "She's not going to—?"

Karma pointed to the sword that Quan held. It looked decidedly closer than a few seconds ago.

Quan wouldn't attack me. Would she? I mean, aside from the blood lessons. She wouldn't try to really kill me with a kamikira?

Fuck.

"Putting it together, are we?" Karma said, getting to her feet and staring at Quan. "I'd say she's been compromised. Wouldn't you? Hold on. Before you answer, let's remove this."

She grabbed Ebonsoul and pulled it from my abdomen— yanked it out would be more accurate. It dematerialized in her hand a moment later. I gasped as white hot agony lanced through me.

"There. Much better don't you think?"

I glared daggers at her as I continued bleeding. My curse didn't work when she paused time.

"You're welcome?" she said, sitting on the edge of the basin and crossing her legs at the ankles. "Oh, that's right. Major wound and no healing. I'll be brief."

"I'd really appreciate it," I said, holding my abdomen. "Brief is good."

"She's been poisoned," Karma said, glancing at Quan. "Can't go into too much detail. No antidote, unless you happen to know the nexus purifier cast?"

"I...I don't."

"Didn't think so. Anyway, seems like her old teacher really knows how to hold a grudge," she said. "She poisoned her and then laid this trap for you. Seems you've made an enemy of her as well. I do have to commend you on your top-notch selection of mortal enemies." She looked at the Phoenix Blade again. "She would have ended you and then died shortly after."

I saw the plan and had to admire the deviousness. Edith was a major threat.

"How?" I asked. "How did she poison her?"

"This is where it gets fascinating," Karma said, leaning in close. "The poison in her body only reacts when exposed to a particular type of blood. That takes brilliance. I'll give you one guess whose blood triggered her poison."

"Mine," I said as pain gripped me. "She needed to be exposed to *my* blood."

"You *are* sharp," she said. "This poison had an added bonus: it came with an embedded command. I'm sure you can figure out what it was."

I looked at Quan holding a god-killing sword and figured it out pretty quickly. Throughout the blood lessons she had been acting strange at key moments.

Every time I'd bled.

"Killing me with that sword," I said. "What kind of poison does that?"

"The kind created by a master venomancer," Karma said. "It does have some devastating applications. Imagine spreading something like that, having mages destroy each other and then bursting into flames. Effective and efficient. If the flame is hot enough, it even cuts down on the cleanup. No bodies to bury, just ash."

"No," I said through clenched teeth. "She doesn't deserve this."

"Are you thinking of saving her?" Karma asked. "She's trying to kill you. Do you not see the trajectory of the sword?"

"I do," I said. "Can I help her?"

Karma looked off to the side and sighed.

"Honestly, Splinter, you can't save her. You can only delay the inevitable. She's done. This is a lost cause."

"Help me."

"I just did," she said, looking around. "You're still here."

"Help me save *her*," I said. "Help me. What poison is it?"

"I told you, there's no antidote."

"What is...what is the poison?"

"The Dragons Breath," she said, and my expression sank. "I told you, Splinter. No antidote. In fact, the moment I leave, she'll lose her abilities and burst into flames a few seconds later. It's going to be positively incendiary."

A thought hit me.

Catalyst, cleansing, and containment. Just like blood. *My* blood.

"Wait," I said. "I need a cup."

"A cup?" Karma asked with a small smile. "A cup for what?"

"My blood."

"You're drinking blood now?" she asked, materializing a

small steel cup. "Have you been spending extra time with your vampire?"

"Not...not for me...for her."

Karma nodded.

"I see," she said, holding the cup to my wound. "*This* is *my* blood lesson for *you*."

"What?" I asked. "What are you talking about?"

"You are willing to save her"—she glanced at Quan—"even when she is actively trying to kill you," she said. "You *are* coming along quite nicely, despite what everyone says."

"I...I don't understand."

"You don't have much time," Karma said, pouring the small cup of my blood into Quan's mouth. "Verity is on its way to extinguish you all...tonight. All you need to know is that Edith doesn't need your blood to *create* the Dragons Breath. She needs it to *negate* it."

"What?"

"Please try to keep up," she said. "The blood of a drag-onblooded immortal is the antidote. She can't very well create a mage-ending subliminal super toxin, and have the antidote running around, alive and all, can she?"

I stared at her in shock.

"I know, it's a lot to process," she continued, tapping me on the cheek without dislocating my jaw. She was probably feeling merciful due to my stomach wound. "We will speak soon...I promise. I'd move back if I were you. Ingesting your blood has some immediate and nasty side effects. Haven't you ever wondered why your vampire never snacked on you?"

I was about to say something when she raised a hand.

"You're welcome," she said. "You have quite a bit to sort out. I'll leave you to it. Remember, move back. Projectile vomit is never pleasant."

"Thank you," I said, managing to drag myself across the floor. "I'm not trying to rush you, but..."

"Right, right, major wound and no healing," she said. "You know, that seems like a design flaw. You should bring that up with Kali, the next time you see her."

I just stared at her.

She disappeared a few seconds later and time snapped back to its normal flow. Quan immediately fell to her knees, dropping the Phoenix Blade and vomiting forcefully across the marble floor. I saw the door to the Crucible open. Monty and Peaches rushed in with Aria and several wordweavers behind them.

The room tilted sideways as I fell back onto the cool marble. I managed to glimpse the orb above the basin. It was a balance of black and gold, surrounded and interlaced with bands of violet.

It was the last thing I saw before the world went black.

TWENTY-SIX

I awoke with a start, feeling for the wound in my abdomen.

"It's healed," Monty said, concern etched on his face. "It was touch and go there for a moment. Aria sorted you straight away. Why did the wound remain open for so long? Doesn't your curse work faster than that?"

"Must have been the poison," I said, giving him the *let's discuss it later* look. "Quan?"

"She had been poisoned," Monty said. "It was a nasty piece of work. From what Aria could determine, it contained a trigger to eliminate you once exposed to enough of your blood. An inevitable circumstance considering the composition of blood lessons."

"How did Edith know?"

"You were poisoned," Monty said. "She knew Quan would attempt blood lessons to deal with the poison. She must have attacked her back at Ellis when they were alone, before your creature saved her. It was a matter of placing the right trigger at the right moment. She almost succeeded too. A few seconds more, and Quan would have used the Phoenix Blade on you."

"There were extenuating circumstances," I said, thinking about Karma. "You know how effective *karma* can be."

Monty gave me a knowing look and nodded.

"I see," he said. "Let's discuss this further when we don't have the threat of impending death on our lives."

"So, basically never?"

"It's good to see you've regained what passes for a sense of humor," Monty said. "I do have to admit that the situation is somewhat dire."

"Somewhat dire is what we specialize in," I said, sitting up. "We can do this."

"We have been in worse straits," he said, brushing off a sleeve. "What I need is a—"

"Strong cup of Deathwish," I said with a grin. "I know. Me too."

He scowled and shook his head.

"Will never happen," he said. "My palate is too sophisticated for coffee."

"Thanks for the rescue," I said with a tight smile, thinking about Quan's words and my designated victim status. "That was close. How long have I been out?"

"About two hours, and don't thank me," Monty said, looking down at my hellhound. "Thank your creature. He made quite the fuss—enough that Aria told him to find you. One petrified wordweaver later, we found the entrance to the Crucible. Well, you know the rest."

"Did he attack the wordweaver?"

"No, but she was frantically trying to get the door to the Crucible open when we arrived," he said. "Apparently, the door had sealed once the blood lessons began. A situation your creature quickly rectified."

"He broke the door?"

"Gently remodeled," Monty corrected. "I smoothed things over with Aria. Its repair will be taken care of if we're around to see another sunrise. Other than the destruction, he was a good boy."

<Thank you, boy>

<Will I get extra meat for finding you? I didn't mean to break the door.>

<I will make sure we go to the place so you can get extra extra. Monty will help them fix the door.>

<Did you eat bad meat too?>

<Something like that. We both need to be careful from now on. We just can't go around eating everything.>

<I don't eat everything. I only eat meat.>

<Well, you need to be careful.>

<I promise to eat everything carefully.>

I realized it was a losing argument and rubbed his head in defeat.

My hellhound rumbled and chuffed.

"How is Quan?"

"She'll recover," Monty said. "Stable, but critical. Whatever you gave her was almost as toxic as the poison she ingested."

"She was exposed to the Dragons Breath," I said. "Edith made it. She has a working version."

His expression darkened.

"How is Quan still alive?" Monty asked. "She should have burst into flames hours ago."

"I gave her the antidote."

Technically it wasn't me, but I wasn't going to go into details right now.

"The antidote?" he said. "The Dragons Breath doesn't have an antidote. It's why Edith is after you, to create—"

"No," I said, cutting him off. "My blood is the antidote. Edith doesn't want my blood to *create* the toxin. She wants to remove me because I'm—"

"The *antidote*," Monty finished. "With you gone, the

Dragons Breath becomes an ultimate weapon. An ultimate toxin with no readily available antidote. Bloody hell."

I nodded.

"I stabilized the poison," I said, extending my arms. The lattice of dark energy was faint and barely noticeable. "Do we still need to do the Rule of Three cast?"

"We can't," Monty said, shaking his head. "Quan is in no condition to cast anything, and I don't know enough of the nexus purifier. Besides, it would seem moot now, don't you think? You've stabilized the poison. The blood lessons were a pretense to isolate and execute you."

"No, they helped me, actually," I said, shaking my head. "Is Verity really on their way?"

"Yes," Monty said. "How did you...? Never mind. We can't mount a counter-offensive, not with a mage toxin in Verity's arsenal."

"We can use my blood to create an antidote," I said. "Is it possible?"

"Yes," said Aria from the doorway. "Not enough for every wordweaver, but enough to demonstrate to Verity who we are."

"How long will it take?" I asked. "Do we have enough time?"

"Enough to prepare a response to Verity," she said. "I hope you're feeling up to the task of donating blood to stop a deranged venomancer from killing thousands of mages."

I nodded.

"Let's do this."

TWENTY-SEVEN

"We have to intercept them before they get here," Monty said. "If they unleash the Dragons Breath on the wordweavers—"

"Verity could wipe them from existence," I said, looking down at a large map of the wordweaver lands and pointing to a location south from the Cloisters. "We can meet them here, at Fort Tryon, to keep them away from the Cloisters."

"They will be forced to bring reduced numbers if Edith decides to unleash the Dragons Breath."

"She'll use it," I said. "Edith and Verity aren't concerned with collateral damage. By now, she thinks Quan and I are dead. They'll attack tonight."

"That works to our advantage," Monty said, looking at where I was pointing on the map. "That location is a ruin. It will be difficult to defend."

"At least they can't blame us for destroying it," I said. "We don't have to hold it, we just need to make them think we are."

Aria looked down at the map.

"It is ideal," she said. "My wordweavers can use Margaret Corbin Drive to fall back here, if needed." She pointed along a long road that led from Fort Tryon to the Cloisters. "The entire complex will be sealed against attack, creating an impenetrable wall."

"We can flank them and trap them against that wall, stopping their attack," I said. "It's a feint into a box canyon."

"This won't end Verity," Aria said, her voice serious. "They are a vast organization, spanning the globe. This operation will garner the attention of the High Tribunal, certainly, but it will not destroy Verity. It will only intensify their animosity toward the two of you."

"Like you said, a battle for another day," I said. "I'm not interested in ending *all* of Verity today, just Edith and the group that's coming for us."

"How many wordweavers do we have?" Monty said, looking out of the window of the Cloisters Tower. We were in Aria's office with a view over the entire wordweaver complex. The sky was a mix of deep orange and pink as the setting sun reflected off the Hudson River. "How many volunteered?"

I had just spent the last three hours donating enough blood to wonder if the plan *was* to exsanguinate me as Monty had said. Aria's words came true. I didn't provide the blood for the Rule of Three cast, but I did make sure that every wordweaver that volunteered for this op had an antitoxin developed with my blood.

"All of them," Aria said, with a slight shake of her head. "But we were only able to create antitoxin for three hundred, the bulk of whom will remain here to protect the others."

"How many are joining us in Fort Tryon?"

"You will have one hundred wordweavers at your back," Aria said. "I will coordinate our defenses here. Your group is mostly comprised of senior weavers, experienced in battle. Your liaison there will be——"

"Me," a voice said from outside the room. "I will lead the wordweavers in the field."

Quan.

I reflexively took a step back.

"Hey," I said, giving her the once-over. "How are you feeling?"

"Better now, thanks to you," she said. "You surpassed all my expectations during your blood lessons. You may not be a mage, but your performance was worthy of any mage I know, myself included."

"Well, it was either pass or die, right?" I said. "Didn't have much of an option."

"I'm...I'm sorry," Quan said. "I was a fool to think I could stand against her. She goaded me with Lyn, and when I attacked, it was too late. If it wasn't for your hellhound, I'd probably be dead right now."

"Twice," I said. "On Ellis and in the Crucible. He found us before it was too late."

"He is an amazing creature," she said, rubbing his head. Then she hesitated, looking at me again. "Thank you. Your blood saved me from the Dragons Breath."

I nodded, making sure to remain serious. If I downplayed it, she would be offended. If I made one of my usual remarks, something along the lines of, *"It was bloody difficult, but we pulled it off"* in my best Monty impersonation, she would be offended.

My options were fairly limited.

Like I said, I was learning.

"It was my honor," I said, with a small bow. "Are you certain you're ready for this tonight?"

She fixed her gaze on the map and nodded.

"Edith must be stopped," she said, her words clipped and full of barely repressed rage. I recognized the tone, because it was similar to my own. "She can't be allowed to use the

Dragons Breath on anyone else."

Monty explained the plan to her as I walked over to the window to catch the last rays of the sun as it dropped below the horizon. A few moments later, Aria came and stood by my side.

I glanced behind us and saw that Monty and Quan had left the office.

"They're off to make preparations," she said. "I wanted a word with you."

I suddenly had a flashback of grade school and being sent to the principal's office for one of my many transgressions. Somehow, he never believed I was innocent of any wrongdoing.

"A word?" I said cautiously. "About?"

"We didn't arrive in time," she said. "Even with your hellhound following your bond and locating you. You should have been killed."

"Time flows differently in the Crucible," I said, keeping my gaze fixed on the view outside the window. "You said so yourself, it's in stasis."

"True," she said, looking out the window. "Except that I had disabled the stasis once I got the alarm from the word-weaver guarding the Crucible."

"It's hard to determine how these things happen," I said. "This world of energy and magic can be unpredictable. At least, that's been my experience."

She turned and gave me a long look, which I ignored. The temperature of the office suddenly went from comfortable to awkward scrutiny in the space of a few seconds. I could feel my face flush under that gaze.

"The poison has stabilized," she said, narrowing her eyes at me. "But this is not what I wanted to discuss with you."

"What did you want to discuss?" I said, turning to her at the tone in her voice. "What is it? Is Verity closer than we thought?"

"Tristan," Aria said, "has been poisoned."

No, no.

"Dragons Breath?"

Aria nodded.

"Give him the antidote! What are we waiting for?"

I made to turn away from the window as she grabbed my arm, rooting me in place. She was surprisingly strong for someone so thin.

"He is safe from the poison. That is not my concern."

"Then?" I asked, confused. "The poison can't hurt him. He's safe."

"Is he?" Aria asked. "I noticed a similarity to Quan when I administered the antidote."

"A similarity?"

"There is a trigger of some kind," she said. "I don't know if the antidote neutralized it or if it will occur at some later time. I don't know what it's keyed to."

"Can't you find out?" I asked. "Isn't there a way?"

"Yes, we ask the person who placed the trigger there in the first place," she said, her face serious. "Do you know who that is?"

I shook my head.

"Edith?"

"Possibly, but there is no way of knowing," she said. "I don't know how he was exposed or how she would embed a command. This is not based on words; this is cause and effect, actions. I am out of my depth."

"It could be anything," I said. "He could activate that trigger and go on a rampage, taking everyone out."

"I doubt it would be that broad of an instruction," Aria

said, staring at me. I looked at her this time and I understood. "She has a very specific target in mind."

"He wouldn't take everyone out," I said. "He would be like Quan."

Aria nodded.

"He would attempt to eliminate you."

TWENTY-EIGHT

"We mobilize in two hours," Aria said. "The evacuation is almost complete."

"Evacuation?" I asked. "I thought most of the force was going to stay back to defend the wordweavers here? Wasn't that the plan?"

"Simon, appear weak when you are strong, and—?"

"Strong when you are weak," I finished. "You want them to come here?"

She nodded and waved a hand as she whispered a word. Her robe transformed into black combat armor, bristling with weapons.

"Where would you prefer to fight for your life? Some strange terrain where you are unsure of your footing, or in your home, where you know every inch of the land?"

"Home, of course," I said. "Won't this make you vulnerable?"

"We will give them a path to follow. By controlling their movements, we control the outcome," she said. "I expect them to arrive soon, once they think our defenses have been weakened."

"Defenses you will weaken deliberately."

"This complex has been designed to withstand a full-scale assault with a dozen or so wordweavers," she said. "We currently have three hundred prepared with antitoxin. I would say the advantage is ours."

"You didn't want to say anything in front of Monty," I said, the realization hitting. "You think he may be compromised."

"There is a possibility, yes," she said, handing me two small vials before heading to the door. "I leave you to prepare. I am going to finish setting our defenses. Our guests will be here soon."

"What's this?" I said, holding up the vials with thick red liquid. "Blood?"

"Antitoxin."

"Um, I don't need—"

"Not for *you*," she said, giving me a withering glare. "There may be others who need it. One vial per person."

"What if I run into a third person and they need the antitoxin?"

"Then I would say it was very fortunate for them to run into *you*, don't you agree?"

I shook my head.

Of course, in an emergency, I could always give someone *my* blood. It would probably destroy their digestive system, but they would be alive.

"I do," I said, putting the vials away in my jacket. "I hope I don't need them."

"If anyone from Verity can be saved, we will save them." She gave me a hard stare. "Plan for every contingency. Even the unthinkable ones."

She left me alone with my thoughts.

I was *not* going to kill Monty.

If we could save Quan, we could save Monty. I just had to figure out what his trigger was.

If I were Monty, how would I try to take me out?

Not that I was trying to brag, but after giving it some thought, I came to the conclusion that I was difficult to kill.

Not impossible, but really, really, difficult.

Still, there were ways.

Stopping time would be one way; it seemed like my curse only worked during the flow of time. If you cut off the flow, you interrupted the curse.

No flow meant no curse, which meant I was mortal and killable. That really did seem like a design flaw, now that I thought about it. Knowing Kali, she probably put that aspect in there deliberately to make my life "interesting".

Interrupt?

Could Monty's Interrupting Palm disrupt Kali's curse? Would it work? How would Edith even know that he had knowledge of the technique to plant a trigger around it?

It would mean she had intimate knowledge of Monty's past and his being a student to Mage Santiago. It was possible but it was thin. Would Ines have shared that with Edith?

I sensed him as he approached.

"Hey, Monty," I said, still thinking about the vials as he entered the room. "Why didn't you tell me?"

"Tell you what?"

"You were poisoned. How did it happen?"

"I'm thinking it was when your creature returned with Quan," he said pensively. "She was covered in blood. It must have been a contact exposure."

"She knew you would be the first to approach Quan," I said, turning over the scene in my head. "Why wasn't I poisoned?"

"You mean aside from your blood?" he asked. "You're not a mage."

"I'm really getting fed up with the whole 'I'm not a mage' comment," I snapped, throwing an arm up in the air. "So what, I'm not a mage? Big deal. I'm not a mage. And?"

He waited until I finished before he continued.

"Done?"

"Yes," I said, letting out a deep breath. "Go on."

"As I was saying," he said, giving me a quick look, "you're not a mage. In this case, that works in your favor. The poison that Edith has created—"

"Dragons Breath?"

"Yes, Dragons Breath," he said. "Targets mages exclusively. Being exposed to Quan's blood would have no effect on you. It's why she is targeting those around you. She can't seem to target you directly."

"Why not use some other kind of poison?" I asked. "Something that would affect anyone, not just mages."

"She probably surmised the same thing as Ines," he said, walking over to the window and looking out over the Hudson. "Kali must be offering you some kind of protection as her Marked One, or else you would be dead by now. Instead of dissuading her, it only—"

"Incentivized Edith to come after me even more."

He nodded.

"Yes, it made you an even greater threat," he said. "One, I daresay, she will try to eliminate, once she realizes Quan failed to dispatch you."

I took a deep breath before speaking again.

"Aria thinks you may have an embedded command since you were exposed to the Dragons Breath."

"Like Quan?"

"Yes, like Quan."

"That would explain her recent standoffishness."

"Is it true?"

"Yes," he said. "I know the trigger."

"Shit," I said "Can you avoid it?"

"Not if I'm to fulfill my vow to Mage Santiago, no."

"The Interrupting Palm."

"Yes," he said, looking down at his hands for a few seconds. "If I use it again, it seems I'm to disrupt your energy signature long enough to render you weak, then—"

"Kill me?"

"I would presume so," Monty said with a nod. "She *really* doesn't like you."

"I'm starting to take this personally."

"You stand in the way of her plan," he said. "She seems determined to usurp Verity. Cain is no threat to her, and Tana is little more than a rabid attack dog from what I understand. A dangerous one, but outmatched and outclassed by Edith's intellect. If she succeeds, she can take control of Verity and challenge the Tribunal."

"Ambitious," I said. "Can she do it?"

"If she possessed control of a mage-killing super toxin, it's very likely, yes."

"What about Ines?"

"She is totally out of her depth," Monty said. "She believes she is serving a greater good."

"Verity is not a greater good," I said. "In fact, Verity and good don't belong in the same sentence...ever."

"Which is why I need to remove her from the Blades and Verity."

"Your plan to do this...it involves the Palm, doesn't it?"

"I'm afraid so."

"So what's the plan?"

"I open Ines' eyes to her true role in Verity," he said, turning to face me. "Her advancement, her position, is a sham, bolstered by her father's legacy and reputation. They are using her to give the Blades credibility. If I can get her to see that, perhaps she will come to her senses."

"Noble," I said. "So...what's the plan?"

"You're not going to like it," he said with a sigh. "It's quite risky."

I matched his sigh.

"In all the time we've worked together, you have yet to hit me with a plan where my response was: 'Yes! That's the plan! Let's do it!' Why start now? Tell me the plan."

"I'll use the Palm to interrupt her signature instead of yours," he said. "It will give Verity the illusion of Ines having lost her abilities, hopefully creating a cascading sequence of events that will force her to face reality."

"Without getting her killed."

"Without getting her killed, yes."

"So we're starting thin," I said. "Familiar territory. Okay, you've activated the trigger. What happens now?"

"Once the trigger is activated, I will seal the energy of the trigger before I lose control."

"Using...the elder blood rune? On yourself?"

"Yes. Meanwhile, as this is occurring, Quan casts the nexus purifier on me."

"To remove the effect of the trigger and help you regain control?"

"Precisely," he said. "The poison is a non-issue due to the antitoxin—thank you, by the way."

"You're welcome," I said. "While all this is happening, what exactly am *I* doing?"

He paused for a few seconds and looked out of the window again.

"Well, you will initiate a stormblood to deal with any potential threats."

"A stormblood?"

"Yes, a stormblood."

"And while we're busy doing all of this casting—out in the open, mind you—what exactly are Edith and Verity doing?"

"I would assume trying to kill us."

I pinched the bridge of my nose as I tried to process the insanity of this plan. We had done some massively dangerous things in the past.

This was par for the course.

That wasn't what concerned me. What concerned me was how easily I accepted that this was the accepted plan of action.

I was concerned I was losing my mind.

"I know you have no sense of humor, but please, please tell me you're joking," I said. "You want to cast some kind of mutated, jumbled-up Rule of Three?"

"If it helps you understand the process, then yes," he said, serious. "It's a Rule of Three cast with a different sequence and a different target."

"That target being you, right?" I asked. "I do have that part right?"

"Yes, you do."

"Quan agreed to this? You told her the entire plan?"

"She was the one who suggested you initiate the stormblood."

"She what? You're both insane."

"I would hazard to say she is further along than I am."

"How are we going to pull off all of that *and* avoid the dying part?" I asked, really worried that Monty had suffered a catastrophic blow to the head somewhere. "Inquiring minds would like to know."

"Well, this is the part you're not going to like," he said.

"Oh, wait, *this* is the part I'm not going to like?" I asked, raising my voice slightly. "You mean, the part you're about to share right now? So, everything up to this part, I should like?"

"You're being dramatic," he said. "Last night, we outraced a disintegrator on the Hudson River. The time for righteous indignation or incredulity has long since passed. Can we move on?"

He was right.

"You may be right," I said, pointing a finger in his face. "Still, I reserve the right to lose my shit when faced with near certain death. What's the part I'm not going to like?"

"You wanted to know how would we be able to do all of this casting while remaining alive, yes?"

"Seems like an important part of the plan, don't you think?"

"You won't just be *initiating* a stormblood," he said. "We will be *casting* a stormblood."

"What the hell, Monty," I said, my voice low. "You've lost your damned mind. The poison did scramble some neurons. Don't you remember what the stormblood did to the forest? The stormblood we had to race away from?"

"I do."

"And you want to cast one here—in a city?"

"We will cast it over the river, and it will be contained."

"Oh, so you're a stormblood-casting expert all of sudden?" I asked, angrily. "How many stormbloods have you cast exactly? In your entire life, how many?"

"You know the answer."

"Damn right I know the answer!" I yelled. "None, that's how many. No, this is beyond insane, even for us, and we are pretty fringe most of the time. This...this is beyond the fringe, and out into the void of the unreal. We can't do this."

"We can and we must."

"No, you don't understand. We *can't* do this," I said. "It will *kill* people. Innocent people will get caught up in the stormblood. Did you forget what Josephine did to those mages? She blasted them to dust. That was the power of the stormblood. And you want to cast that? What are you thinking? Does Aria know about this plan?"

"No," he said, letting out another sigh. "Her only concern are her wordweavers, as it should be. *We* have to look at the larger picture when others can't or won't."

"All I'm seeing in the larger picture right now is death. Lots of it. Starting with the two of us."

"If Edith manages to capture or kill you, she will be unstoppable. Verity will fall first, but it won't stop there. She will subvert every magical organization on the planet. Every single one. Right now, we are the only obstacle to her plans."

I shook my head.

"Call Dex, call the Dark Council," I said, trying to find a solution. "We can call Hades. Maybe even Ezra. Let's get the sects involved somehow. There has to be another way."

"Take a breath," he said, keeping his voice calm. "All of those are excellent suggestions, except for one thing."

"What?"

"Edith and Verity are on their way here *tonight*," he said, looking out over the Hudson again. "We don't have the time to rally forces to stop Verity. She's counting on that. Time is against us."

"Fuck," I said. "Why are we always the last line of defense?"

"Because it's what we do and who we are," he said. "If we don't stop her here, tonight, no mage will be able to stand against her."

I took a long breath and let it out, gazing out over the Hudson.

"It's a good thing I'm not a mage, then."

TWENTY-NINE

I was about to say more when I sensed another presence by the door. I raised a hand as the wordweaver silently entered the room. Monty gave me a puzzled look, but nodded.

"Your presence is requested at the central cuxa," she said with a slight nod in my direction. "It would seem you have a guest."

"*I* have a guest?"

"Yes. Would you like an escort to the cuxa?"

"Considering I don't know what a cuxa is and the corridors here have a habit of appearing and disappearing, yes, I would like an escort."

"Good choice."

"Edith is setting everything in motion," Monty said. "Stay alert."

The wordweaver led us down several corridors, and we finally ended up in the central courtyard where we'd met Aria when we first arrived.

The wordweaver bowed silently and stepped away, leaving us alone in the courtyard. It looked much different at night.

It still felt tranquil, but now, in the darkness, it held a subtle threat, a promise of danger.

Monty disappeared from sight, but I could still sense his energy signature close by.

"So, cuxa means courtyard," I said, mostly to myself. "Who knew?"

"I did," a voice said in the darkness off to my side. "Hello, Simon."

Ines.

I let my hand drop to Grim Whisper as she raised both of hers.

"What are you doing here?" I said. "You tried to melt me with your disintegrator orb of death. I didn't appreciate it. Plus, we killed the *Mobula* because of you. Do you know how pissed Cecil is going to be when he finds out?"

"Mobula?" she asked. "Who's Cecil?"

"Not important," I said, waving her words away. "What do you want?"

"I'm here to discuss the terms of your surrender," she said, lowering her hands slowly. I kept mine on the holster of Grim Whisper. "Every action I've taken has been in my capacity as an agent of Verity."

"The terms of my...what?" I asked with a small laugh. "Now I know you've lost your mind. Listen, I've had a rough few days. Why don't you go back to your psycho venomancer and tell her I said fuck you very much, but no. There will be no surrendering tonight. Unless you want to surrender to me?"

"You have no idea what you are up against," she said. "Verity is more than just one mage. We span the planet. There is nowhere—literally nowhere—you can go, that we can't find you."

"I'm touched, but my answer still stands: no thank you."

"You're making this an emotional issue when it doesn't need to be."

"Oh, I'm sorry," I said. "I tend to have emotional responses when people want to *kill* me. I'm special that way."

She brushed off a sleeve in an eerily Montaguean gesture and I shuddered at the similarity.

"It's not personal," she said impassively. "I'm simply executing the edicts of the High Tribunal."

"That sounds like a sophisticated version of the 'I'm just following orders' line of B.S.," I said. "Didn't work out so well in the past, won't work now."

"Edith plans to kill every wordweaver in this complex," she said, looking around slowly. "You can prevent that."

"How did you even get in here?" I asked. "Does Aria know you're here?"

"Do you really think I'm strong enough to breach the defenses of this complex on my own?" Ines asked. "Of course she knows I'm here. She wants to prevent senseless deaths just as much as I do."

"Really?" I asked. "Aria risked her wordweavers to allow you entrance?"

The words were right, but her body language yelled of lies. I wouldn't put it past Aria to give Verity a false sense of security; she could be devious in her own way. Still, it felt off.

"She allowed me to enter," Ines insisted. "Just me."

Of course. Aria providing the enemy a path to their own destruction

"What do you really want?" I asked. "What does Verity want?"

"Peace."

That's when I laughed out loud. I held up a hand as I gathered myself.

"Peace?" I said, still chuckling. "That's ironic. I didn't really get a sense of *peace* when Verity chased us up the river.

It was still missing when you tried to capsize us. And it was definitely nowhere to be seen when you tried to melt us with your death orb."

"Again, you're making this personal. It's not."

"Let's try this again," I said, my voice serious. "What does Verity want? Don't you dare say peace again."

"In a word, you," Ines said. "Edith wants you. She's willing to call off this entire attack if you come with me."

"You're either new to this, extremely naive, or some combination of both," I said. "Edith isn't going to call off anything. I've dealt with her kind before. Wake up. This is a zero-sum game."

"She is willing to extend you safe passage to her ship," she said. "In exchange, she will leave this wordweaver complex and every wordweaver unharmed."

"That's mighty generous of her," I said, feeling my hell-hound blink in next to me with a low rumble. I reached down and scratched behind his ears without taking my eyes off Ines. "Did she tell you why? Why I'm so important?"

Ines' face darkened for a moment.

"No," she said. "Edith doesn't share the details of her plans with me. She holds considerable sway over the High Tribunal and acts with operational autonomy. She usually gets what she wants."

I bet.

The High Tribunal wasn't suicidal enough to get on Edith's bad side. Not when she had a super toxin that could target mages. I had a suspicion that even Archmages were vulnerable to the Dragons Breath.

"You're third-in-command, and yet Edith can determine to end this attack just like that?"

"Yes," Ines said. "That is how much influence she wields."

"She outranks you?"

"She is currently the acting leader of the Blades," Ines

answered after some hesitation. "Yes, she outranks me."

It seemed that aside from the Tribunal, Edith wielded real power now that Cain had been sidelined. It probably meant that she was the real force behind the Blades, not Tana.

"Why isn't Tana here trying to negotiate my surrender?" I asked. "She's the second-in-command. Seems like that would be the play, not sending the third-in-command. No offense."

"Tana is...volatile," Ines said with a sigh. "She's not particularly known for her negotiating skills."

"She lacks tact and diplomacy?"

"You could say that," Ines said. "She'd rather unleash death than have a conversation that can prevent it."

"And Edith?"

"Edith is after power," Ines said. "She would prefer to end this conflict without bloodshed, if possible."

"Somehow, I doubt that," I said. "I think you're missing some important information."

"Such as?"

"She would prefer no bloodshed as long as she gets her hands on my blood, that is," I said. "Haven't you wondered why?"

"What would you give to save those around you?" she asked, ignoring my question. "All of these lives rest in your hands. Would you put your life above theirs? Would you risk them all to save yourself?"

I thought back to Monty trying to convince her to leave Verity. It was going to be harder than he thought, but it was worth a try. Let's see how much Verity Kool-Aid she had drank.

"Why don't you come join us?" I asked, moving my hand from Grim Whisper. "You have to know Edith's intentions are less than honorable."

That's putting it mildly.

"Verity exists to police mages," she said. "We exist to

maintain order, to protect and to serve the magical community around the world. How could you possibly understand? You're not a mage. I don't know what you are."

"Most don't," I said with a small smile. "Do you really think Verity needs *you*? That you are some essential part of the machine?"

"I'm third-in-command of the Blades," she said with a hint of pride. "Of course Verity needs me."

"It's been my experience that when groups like Verity get to a certain size, the members—like you—start wearing red shirts," I said. "Know what I mean?"

"No, I don't," she said. "I'm here to broker peace."

"Unlikely," I heard Monty say as he materialized and stepped up behind me. "Edith used you to try and breach the defenses here."

"She would never..." Ines said, looking off to the west. "No."

"Yes," Monty said. "Even now Verity agents are scaling the west wall while others are approaching from the south. Feel free to see for yourself."

Ines closed her eyes, and in that moment Monty moved. I want to say he dashed over to where she stood, but that would be too slow. He teleported to where she stood, and struck her with the Interrupting Palm.

"Perfect," another voice said from behind us. "I knew you wouldn't be able to resist. The hero complex runs too strong in your family. You just had to save her, didn't you?"

Edith emerged from the shadows, giving off major Emperor Palpatine vibes.

Her black hair was pulled back in a tight braid which hung behind her. Instead of the gray robe, she wore a dark burgundy mageiform suit. A blood-red phoenix adorned one side of her rune-covered suit, glowing with subtle shades of red.

Her pale skin still shone with an inner energy, and her expression was one of barely controlled rage, with madness hovering around the edges. A small smile formed across her lips, but it never reached her eyes, which were now two black pits of darkness.

"I like the eyes," I said, taking a step back. "Is that what you call night vision?"

"You?" she said. "Why are you not dead?"

"I like to channel my inner cockroach," I said, still moving back. "I heard they can survive a nuke."

"Quiet," she said and waved a hand in my direction. "I'll deal with you in a moment."

The wave of kinetic energy that hit me slammed me back into one of the columns across the courtyard. I heard the crack of my arm before I fell to the ground. My body flushed with heat, healing me almost instantly—so fast, in fact, that I barely had a moment to register the pain.

That's new.

I remained motionless and let my senses expand. Monty was right: Verity agents were scaling the west wall and approaching from the south. What they weren't expecting, were the squads of wordweavers hidden in Fort Tryon Park.

The sound of fighting and magical attacks filled the park a few moments later.

"You," Edith said, pointing to Monty. "Kill Strong. Now."

Monty looked dazed as he approached my location. For a few seconds, judging from his expression, I thought he was really coming over to finish me off.

"My power," Ines said, looking down at her hands. "What did you do?"

"He erased you," Edith said, narrowing her eyes at Ines. "Your abilities are gone. You are worthless to me in this state."

"No," Ines said. "He couldn't have. How?"

"Does it matter?" Edith spat. "You have served your purpose. We gained access to the complex. Your job here is done. You provided a path for the breach. I will make sure you receive the highest commendations—posthumously, of course."

"What?" Ines snarled, turning to Edith. "I can recover my power. I'm third-in-command. I'm—"

"What you are is a nuisance, and irrelevant," Edith said. "Don't you understand? Verity doesn't need you. *I* don't need you. You have no place in *my* Verity."

"*Your* Verity?" Ines repeated. "What are you saying?"

It was sad to watch Ines' world crumbling around her as reality set in. I really hoped Monty had a plan to help her recover—that is, if we survived the night.

Edith turned away from Ines for a moment.

"Montague, why isn't he dead?" she called out. "Are you stalling?"

"Once she attacks," Monty said, his voice strained as he fought the compulsion of the trigger, "I'll have to cast the rune of sealing. You'll be on your own for a while."

"On my own?" I asked. "For how long?"

"Quan is on her way," he said, falling to one knee as he struggled against the trigger. "Once Quan casts the purifier, initiate the stormblood."

"I don't know *how* to initiate the stormblood," I hissed. "No one ever showed me how—"

"You passed the blood lessons," he said, as blood began pouring from his eyes and ears. "You know how. Remember the lessons."

He began gesturing as Edith focused on him.

"You really are trying to fight the trigger?" Edith said with that smile of malice across her lips. "How adorable. Still, what a waste. I had such plans for you. Dexter will be furious." A small laugh escaped her lips. "It's the small victories that make it all worthwhile. Goodbye, Mage Montague."

She flicked a wrist and sent a black orb of energy at Monty. The orb punched into his chest and launched him out of the courtyard, into an adjacent corridor with a wet crunch.

My chest became tight with fear.

"You bitch," Ines hissed. "You didn't have to kill him."

"Oh, but I did," Edith said. "You see, his uncle and I have *history*. Violent, dark, and unrelenting history. I'm just getting started."

I sensed the subtle energy of the elder rune of sealing and knew Monty was alive. I breathed out a sigh of relief.

That relief was short lived.

Peaches rumbled—Edith was turning her focus to me.

"Shh," I said, rubbing his head. "Not yet. Not yet."

Ines screamed and threw a dagger at Edith.

Edith caught it by the blade without even looking in Ines' direction.

Shit. She isn't just a venomancer. Edith is a major threat.

"A knife?" Edith said, turning back to Ines, who faced her defiantly. "You threw a knife at me, you stupid child?"

"The High Tribunal will erase you," Ines said. "Verity is not yours."

"The High Tribunal?" Edith scoffed. "I *own* the High Tribunal, the cowards. By the time I'm done, they will bow before me. They all will."

"You sick, deluded fu—" Ines never got to finish her sentence.

Edith waved a hand in her direction and shoved her up and out of the courtyard. Over the west side.

<Go get her, boy. Take her to the room where you found me downstairs, then come back.>

Peaches rumbled and blinked out as I stood.

It was just me and Edith now.

THIRTY

"You have proven to be more of a headache than I anticipated," she said. "Like a splinter under a nail. You are an annoying little shit worthy of extermination."

I smiled at her use of "splinter." Karma would be proud.

I gave Edith a small bow, took a deep breath and stepped forward. I was about to do what I did best.

Push mage buttons.

"Wow, for such a powerful assassin, you really suck at your profession," I said, while mentally rushing Quan to the courtyard to cast the purifier. "How many times did you try to ice me?"

"More than once," Edith said. "Which is one time too many."

"Yet I'm still here," I said, forming Ebonsoul. The little voice in my head was screaming at me that this was a BAD IDEA. I slapped some duct tape across his mouth and shoved him into the closet along with any sense of reason I still possessed. "What is it, exactly? Too scared to take matters into your own hands? All this power, and you can't kill me?"

"It's not *can't*, Strong," she said, forming two short blades similar to Ebonsoul, but lacking the runes. "It's *won't*. I prefer your blood in your body, but I'm prepared to adapt to new levels of inconvenience. I *only* need your blood. I don't need the rest of you."

"Sounds like you're scared," I said, moving to the center of the courtyard. "First, that convoluted plan with Quan... Total overkill, by the way. You've never heard about keeping it simple, *stupid?* Way too many moving parts."

And yet it nearly succeeded.

"You know, now that you mention it, simplicity is usually the best course of action," she said, raising her weapons and admiring them. "I'm going to remove your arms first, then your legs. That will prevent you from escaping. I'm also going to remove your tongue, because I simply cannot stand to hear you prattle on any longer. That simple enough for you?"

"I'm sorry?" I said, as I turned to face her again. "Were you saying something? I was distracted by the fact that your ships on the river are getting blasted to bits."

Aria was living up to her word. She was keeping the word-weaver complex safe by destroying and sinking Verity ships on the Hudson.

Edith didn't even shift her glance.

"There are more ships on the way," she said. "What's a few ships in the grand scheme of things?"

"You don't care about your Verity agents?"

"I am Verity," she said. "There is no Verity without me. The agents exist to die for me. That is their purpose."

We had officially entered megalomaniac country and I was standing at the crossroads of Delusion and Grandeur. I knew she was deluded—I just hadn't realized *how* deluded. If she had control of the Dragons Breath, no magic-user was safe.

She would kill every mage.

Edith laughed, then, and I felt fear for the first time.

"You finally understand," she said. "I am inevitable. Once I end you, I will hold ultimate power in my hands."

"The important part of that statement," I said, stepping into a defensive stance, and hoping she was arrogant enough to meet me on my terms, "is that you need to end me first. Can you?"

I was counting on the fragility of mages and their egos. In actuality, she had nothing to prove to me. She could unleash another of her kinetic waves and bounce me all over the courtyard until I was a broken and bloody mess, then finish me off with a killing blow.

Pride. Arrogance.

According to Einstein, the only thing more dangerous than ignorance was arrogance. I had learned this long ago. Those who wield the most power had the thinnest skins; they were easily provoked, and easily manipulated.

I may not have been a mage. I didn't wield immense levels of power or energy, but I possessed one thing very few mages did.

An acceptance of my limitations.

I knew stepping into a fight with Edith was madness. I was going to get cut, I was going to bleed, but I knew my limitations. Fighting her with Ebonsoul was insane, yes. Trying to go toe to toe with her using my magic missile was suicide.

I knew my limitations.

I could last longer facing her blades than trying to blast her with waves of energy. It wasn't going to be much longer—I had no illusions about her skill compared to mine—but even if it was a few seconds longer, it could make all the difference.

When it came to life and death, a few seconds might be all anyone needs.

"I'm going to kill you and see if Kali's Marked One is truly favored."

She still didn't know about my curse—good.

One more advantage in my favor. I would take every advantage I could get.

She closed the distance patiently, cutting off angles until I had no choice but to engage. I immediately understood that she was better than me...if I fought properly.

She lunged forward to impale me on one of her blades, and several things happened at once. I sensed Quan appear next to Monty. Edith must have sensed her, too, because she lost her concentration for a split second.

"You," she said, glancing to where Monty lay. "I'll kill you next, my apprentice, and this time I'll make sure to end you."

In the next moment, I felt a surge of energy as Quan cast what I could only assume was the nexus purifier. As soon as the energy from the purifier filled the courtyard, my hellhound blinked in and latched on to Edith's leg, chomping down hard. She screamed in a rage, backhanding him off her leg and sending him flying into Fort Tryon Park.

Through our bond, I sensed that he had blinked out and reappeared in the park, safely. Hellhounds were truly indestructible.

In that smallest of windows, where Edith's attention was pulled in so many directions, I lunged forward. Even distracted as she was, she saw my attack and twisted her body, bringing one of her blades around to impale me in the side.

She reacted just half a second too late.

Ebonsoul cut through her suit as if it were made of tissue. It sliced through the layers and runes, and plunged into her side, just under her ribs.

As far as attacks went, I would have preferred plunging my blade into her heart, but I feared she didn't have one and the attack would've been wasted. So I opted for safe instead of dramatic.

Her attack sliced into my jacket and stopped short of my skin. I sent Piero a silent prayer for his insistence on my wearing runed jackets and rolled back, bracing myself as I sensed the wave of kinetic energy build around her.

It felt like watching the ocean during a storm.

Around her, I sensed the energy build, rising higher and higher, surrounding us. I saw the stones and pebbles around the courtyard begin to float around her.

She grabbed her side as she bled freely, and growled at me.

"I'm going to kill everyone you know," she said, her voice low. "Then I'm going to kill everyone they know, and everyone they know, until there is no one alive who will dare utter your name. Then, and only then, am I going to kill you."

As threats went, it was in the top ten, maybe even the top five. I mean, it didn't displace, *"You tell them I'm coming and hell's coming with me,"* but it was a definite contender.

I did the last thing she expected—which, if you knew me, was the most expected thing.

I laughed.

"Do you know who I am?" I asked, as the energy of my siphon slammed into my body, filling me with power. "I am your end."

THIRTY-ONE

She released the wave of kinetic energy.

It tore a trench in the marble as it crossed the courtyard. I sensed Monty and Quan next to me as the power in me multiplied. Monty leaned on my shoulder and nodded as Quan gestured and formed a white circle on the ground underneath us.

I looked at her and she nodded at me.

The circle began to glow brightly as I reached in and found the stormblood that linked me to Monty. The blood lessons came back to me.

Frequency.

I sensed the storm of lightning and power inside of me, fueled by rage, and removed all barriers. Arcs of power danced around our bodies, jumping from me to Monty to Quan and back again. I could sense the clouds roll in, even if I couldn't see them. The night became just that much darker as the power grew around us.

Structure.

Everything was connected; I unleashed my innersight and saw. All around me, I saw the symbols, interconnected, linked with one another. Circles and diagrams floated before me, rotating slowly and morphing from one shape to another and back again. There was no distinction, and there was every distinction.

Execution.

Energy couldn't be destroyed, but it could be transformed.

I reached out with both arms and absorbed the kinetic energy Edith had unleashed. As I grabbed hold, my knees buckled. Monty and Quan grabbed my arms, holding me up. I took Edith's energy and reshaped it, making it mine, ours, transforming it into something wild, something feral, something ancient and unknowable. It was power, raw power. I stood in its presence and accepted how small I was before it. I was a grain of sand before a mountain of power.

I released it, and unleashed the stormblood.

I sagged back into Quan's arms as Monty stepped forward, lightning coruscating around his body. He extended an arm into the sky as the Verity agents scaled over the west wall. I pushed off Quan and extended a hand at them. I was going to give them the jolt of their lives and send them back over the wall and into the water below.

Lightning cascaded around me as blue-white bolts shot forward. The Verity agents never stood a chance. The bolts incinerated them where they stood.

One moment they had come over the wall, the next they were piles of ash. All around us, everything had grown still. I could sense every mage around us. Every mage and word-weaver in the park. Every Verity agent on the river. All of them were within reach. With a thought, I could direct power at them.

"Impossible," Edith cried out. "You're not a mage! You're not strong enough!"

Monty paused in his approach and looked back at me and Quan.

"No, he isn't a mage," he said, turning back to face her. "He is so much more."

Edith regained her wits and threw up a shield, followed by a barrier, which was surrounded by a lattice of black and red energy. Monty looked past her to the river.

I followed his gaze with my eyes, seeing what he could see through our connection in the storm blood. We would show her what it meant to wield power—what it meant to feel fear.

Monty looked back at me and I nodded.

He outstretched a hand at the river.

A bolt of energy raced across the surface of the Hudson. It sliced through all of the Verity ships in one pass. It was a bolt of power and devastation, unmerciful, unforgiving, and unstoppable.

I sensed the Verity agents diving into the water as their ships sank.

Edith was gesturing furiously behind her barricades. Fear was etched on her face as Monty returned his attention to her. Blue energy filled his eyes as he gazed on her.

"You wanted to kill us," Monty said, his words trembled as he spoke. "You have passed judgment upon us."

"As is my authority!" Edith answered from behind her defenses. "I am the leader of Verity. I am Verity. You are too dangerous to let live!"

"You are a murderer, a usurper, and a traitor," Monty said as more electrical energy gathered around him. "We pass judgment on you."

"Death," I whispered, before Monty glanced at me.

"Death," he repeated, and then said it much louder. "Death!"

Thunder rumbled across the skies as lightning strikes hit the courtyard all around us. Quan gestured again, reinforcing the circle around us, but I knew, or part of me knew, that the power wouldn't harm us. We controlled the power. It obeyed us.

"DEATH," Monty said as he raised an arm and brought it down suddenly.

He stumbled back as Quan and I caught him. We were still inside her circle, surrounded by silence.

For a few seconds, everything paused.

It reminded me of being on an open field, right before a major storm. The air all around us was charged and I could feel the energy in the air. Thunder rumbled above us.

I looked up, but there was nothing to see except bolts of energy racing across the clouds. I looked back down and focused on Edith.

Edith sneered behind her defenses.

"Nothing," she spat. "You are nothing and you will *always* be nothing. You insignificant, pathetic excuse for a mage." She waved an arm around and started laughing. "You will never cast again after tonight. This is all sound and fury, signifying—"

The largest bolt of lightning I had ever seen descended into the courtyard, completely engulfing us. Edith was rendered to ash in the space of a thought, and then that ash was disintegrated further—into nothingness.

"Nothing," Monty said. "That is what she is now."

I was about to step out of the circle when Quan grabbed me by the arm and shook her head.

"Look," she said, her voice tight. "It's still going."

Lightning strikes, smaller than the one that had just blasted Edith to atoms, were still hitting the river. Some of them had hit the Cloisters Tower with no damage. That's when I started noticing the pattern.

"They're getting closer," I said with a sick feeling in my stomach. "It looks like they're headed—"

"Right for us," Monty finished. "I don't suppose either of you know how to stop a stormblood?"

"What in the bloody blazes were you thinking, lad?"

It was Dex.

A very pissed-off Dex was standing in front of our circle with his arms crossed, glaring at Monty and me.

"Do you know what you have done?" Dex continued, as he batted away a lightning strike heading his way, sending it into a nearby wall and blowing chunks of stone into the air. "You cast a bloody stormblood in the city!"

He was dressed in a black suit with green accents, and I could see light green runes pulsing along the surface of his suit.

"Can you stop it?" Monty asked. "I'd rather it not create collateral damage or harm innocents."

"Oh, you'd rather not," Dex said, raising his voice. "Where was that consideration when you cast the bloody thing? If it crosses over the river, it will decimate the population over there." He pointed across the Hudson to New Jersey. "That blood will be on your hands. The both of you."

I remained silent, realizing my "I'm not a mage" defense was shaky at best.

"Can we do anything to stop it before that happens?" I asked. "Anything?"

"You?" Dex snarled and fixed me with a glare. "You two have done plenty, don't you think?"

"If there's anything we can do to stop—"

"I said, you've done enough." Dex said, his voice laced with death. "I'm bringing an expert. Now shut your mouths, and let her clean up your mess."

He disappeared in a green flash.

"Her," I said, looking at Monty. "He didn't?"

"He did," Monty said with a nod. "I think it would be best to heed his advice. Say nothing. I mean it."

Another green flash blinded us a few seconds later and Dex reappeared. Next to him, I could feel the energy coming off of her in waves, suppressing the circle we stood in.

Josephine.

"Where are they?" she asked.

Dex pointed to us standing in Quan's circle of protection. Josephine waved a hand and Quan's circle vanished, exposing us to the full fury of the stormblood we had cast.

"You should feel the consequences of your actions," Josephine said. "Don't you agree?"

Monty, Quan and I merely nodded, saying nothing. Each of us held onto one of the columns around the courtyard to prevent being blown out into the river by the cutting wind. Every so often, a lightning strike would hit the courtyard, electrical energy spider-webbing across the ground before disappearing.

Josephine stood in the center of the courtyard, eyes closed as the full force of the stormblood raged around her. After a few seconds, she opened her eyes and looked in our direction. She undid the ponytail holding her hair back.

The wind blew her hair around, and she smiled before growing serious again and looking off into the distance.

"You," she said, pointing at Quan, "are needed elsewhere."

With a wave of her hand, a blue-white circle formed under Quan and disappeared her from sight.

"You have to admit," Josephine said, turning to a still-angry Dex standing unmovable in the middle of the wind, "it's quite impressive for their first." She turned to us and winked. "You always remember your first."

"Ach, do *not* encourage them, woman," Dex growled. "They already have Verity after them. This is only going to make things worse."

"Verity is worse than the Consortium," she said with a

wave of her hand. "This wind is getting annoying. I can barely hear myself think."

She gestured and the wind stopped so suddenly, it was disorienting.

"Ah, there," she continued. "Much better."

The silence was deafening.

I looked around, and much to my surprise, there was no damage to the courtyard or the Cloisters itself. Whatever defenses Aria had in place were working overtime.

"There's still that to address," Dex said, pointing up at the roiling clouds above us. "Before the strikes start fires would be best."

"You have to loosen up a bit, Dexter," Josephine said, wiggling her bare feet in the grass next to the courtyard. "Don't you think we should give them a chance to undo the stormblood? Next time we may not—"

"Next time?" Dex said, staring daggers at Monty and me. "There will be no next time until they learn how to control this infernal thing flawlessly. Is that understood?"

Monty and I both nodded. It didn't seem wise to share any words at the moment. Dex looked like he was ready to pull out Nemain and start cutting us down to size.

"Very well," Josephine said with a huff. "Pay close attention. Foundation, structure, and execution. You follow?"

"Yes," I said. "Catalyst, cleansing, and containment."

"Very good," she said. "See? They're learning."

Even Dex gave me a grudging nod.

"Aye, learning how to destroy is easy," Dex snapped. "Any rank amateur can tear a place apart. You two have proven that many times over. Rebuilding, restoring...that is the path to mastery." He stared at me. "What is the order now? How do you restore the balance? How do you stop the stormblood?"

Josephine stepped back and crossed her arms with a smile and nodded at me.

"You remove the catalyst," I said, giving it some thought. "Drain the storm of its energy."

"Well?" Dex said, looking at Monty. "What are you waiting for? A bloody invitation?" Dex pointed up. "Get to removing."

Monty looked up and took a deep breath before gesturing.

Dex and Josephine both looked up. I followed their gaze and saw an enormous orb of gray energy descend from the clouds. It was easily the size of a truck, and I could see Monty straining to keep it under control. It looked like he was having difficulty holding the orb in place.

"Well done," Josephine said. "You may want to let it go."

"Not over the city," Dex added. "That would be catastrophic."

Monty guided the orb over the Hudson and dropped it into the river. It floated down into the water, reminding me of the orb Aria had dropped into the pool. A moment later, a massive explosion detonated, shooting a column of water into the air.

"Bah! Effective, but sloppy," Dex said, scrunching up his face. "Finesse and nuance, lad. Not everything has to explode.

Then, "Next!" Dex barked at me. "We don't have all night."

"Cleansing," I said. "Remove anything foreign to the remaining structure to restore balance."

Josephine nodded her with pride.

"Well?" Dex said, looking at Monty, who was already gesturing. "I'm not getting any younger."

Monty, who was sweating considerably by now, kept gesturing as symbols floated into the clouds above us. Slowly, all of the clouds started to break apart, leaving a clear night sky.

"Acceptable," Dex said, then looked at me. "What now?"

"Containment," I said, looking up. "You reverse the execution, transforming the energy into another form."

"Close," Dex said, walking over to the where an image of Quan's circle remained. "Convert the energy to its earlier state, rendering the cast inert. I'll handle this one, nephew. You're looking a bit peaked."

Monty sagged with relief. He looked worn out. I figured it was the back to back casting after facing off against Edith.

Dex stepped over to the circle Quan had created and crouched down, placing a hand in its center. A blast of wind shot upward into the night sky, and the circle slowly vanished.

"That was exciting," Josephine said with a smile.

Dex gave her a low growl.

"I mean, you should never do that again," Josephine added with mock seriousness. "If you do intend to unleash another stormblood, I suggest paying me a visit first." Another low growl from Dex. "In order to hone your stormblood skills, of course—not to unleash stormbloods willy-nilly in my forest. We must have a modicum of control, after all. Isn't that right, Dexter?"

"Thank you, Josephine," Dex said, creating a large green circle in the courtyard under her. "That will be all."

"One more thing," she said, motioning for me to draw close. She leaned closer to me when I approached the edge of the circle. "You took life with your stormblood. Do you remember my words?"

I remembered the Verity agents who had scaled the west wall, and her words came back to me: *Heed my words, Marked of Kali. The time will come when you will have done far worse than this.*

"Yes," I said with a short nod. "I remember."

"Good," she said. "You make certain to remember each one. It should never be indiscriminate. Each one will stay with you, for as long as you live—which, in your case, will be quite some time."

She looked at Dex and nodded.

Another blinding green flash, and Josephine was gone.

THIRTY-TWO

Aria approached us with Ines trailing behind her.

"Well met, Dexter," Aria said with a bow. "I offer you my thanks for protecting my wordweavers and our complex."

"Ach, lass," Dex said, waving her words away, "the honor is mine." He glared at Monty and me. "It's the least I can do on account it was my kin which caused you the aggravation to begin with. What is the blood debt owed?"

It was the first I had heard of a blood debt.

"None," Aria said, looking at Monty and then me. "We lost no wordweavers this evening, and I have gained a new apprentice."

Aria stood to the side and motioned to Ines to step forward.

"You joined the wordweavers?" I asked. "Is that allowed?"

"Yes," Aria said. "She will learn our ways, and in time her abilities will return. We will reshape them to conform to her new purpose as a wordweaver. Simon, I believe you have something that belongs here?"

"I do?" I asked, looking around and then patting my pockets. "I don't think so."

Aria whispered a word and the vials of antitoxin appeared in her hand.

"Oh, those," I said. "Good idea. They'll be safer here with you."

"We don't know if Edith shared the knowledge of the Dragons Breath," Aria said. "With this, we can create more. In the future, we may need you to pay us a visit for a...donation."

"Of course," I said. "Whenever I'm not fighting for my life or trying to protect this city, I'll drop by."

"Please, do," Aria said with a smile, then grew serious. "Tristan, I want to offer you my deepest apologies. There are times when those of us who are older fail to accept that we too can learn from those who are younger. I did not place my trust in you when it mattered, and for that, I will make amends." She produced a silver card and handed it to Monty. It disappeared from view a second later. "The wordweaver library is open to you at any time."

Monty bowed deeply.

"My deepest thanks," Monty said, and I realized this was a big deal. "I will strive to honor this gift."

"Really?" I said, not seeing why this was so amazing. "She basically gave you a library card and told you to come visit whenever you want. Granted, it's a glorified library card, but it's still a library card. I mean, really?"

"Simon," Monty said, "it's not just a library card. I'll explain later."

"There is one more thing," Aria said. "Tristan, please form an orb of power."

Monty extended his hand and focused.

Nothing happened.

He tried again and nothing happened.

"Was it the stormblood?" I asked. "Maybe that has something to do with it."

"What was the trigger?" Aria asked gently. "The one that Edith used against you."

"The Interrupting Palm," Monty said, and Dex hissed. "What is it?"

"Did you use the complete technique?" Dex asked. "Both of them?"

"Both of them?" Monty asked, confused. "I used only the Interrupting Palm. What are you referring to?"

"The Connecting Palm," Dex said. "Too much of one creates an imbalance. You have to use both. Usually in sequence."

"She knew I didn't know the other half of the technique," Monty said. "She said it. I will never cast again after tonight. That was her plan all along. It wasn't to kill you." He looked at me. "It was to neutralize my abilities."

"How?' I asked shocked. "How did she do it?"

"She must have known about my knowledge of the Palm technique," Monty said. "I certainly didn't tell her."

"She knew," Ines said. "After our fight at the dock, she asked me how you beat me. I told her about the technique. I didn't know she could use it as a trigger."

"It must have been a timed activation or I wouldn't have had access to my abilities during the stormblood," Monty said. "There was a delay in the neutralizing of my access."

"What about Ines?" I said, looking at Aria. "You said she would get her abilities back. Can't that be the same for Monty?"

Monty shook his head, a bitter laugh escaping his lips.

"Ines wasn't the caster, I was," he said. "Whatever Edith did to transform her poison severed my ability to access energy. She used the energy of the palm to interrupt my access."

"She broke your magic?"

"My connection to it, yes."

"There is a solution," Dex said. "You have to find a mage who can teach you the other half of the technique. The Connecting Palm."

"Did Mage Santiago ever mention another part of the technique?" I asked. "Something he may have said while he was teaching you the Interrupting Palm?"

"I never heard him mention another palm technique," Monty said. "If he knew it, he never shared it with me."

We all turned to Ines.

"I heard him talk about a Restoring Palm once," she said. "Once, when I was a little girl, he was speaking to some other mages in the Golden Circle. He didn't know I could overhear their conversation."

"What did he say?" Monty asked. "What was the Restoring Palm?"

"My father said he would never teach it to anyone," Ines said. "It was too dangerous and needed to disappear from the face of the earth. Too much damage had been done with it."

"Did he ever mention if anyone taught it?" I asked. "Another member of your family, maybe? Did he teach it to anyone else?"

"No," she said. "I am sorry. It was the only time I ever heard of that technique. I had no idea it was connected to the Interrupting Palm."

"What happens to Monty?" I asked, glancing at him. "Will he be okay? I mean, besides not being able to access energy?"

"He will start to age," Dex said. "Slowly, at first, and then faster. Even though he can't access it, the energy within will sustain him, until it doesn't. When that happens, the aging will accelerate. After that, there's not much that can be done."

"Someone else has to know about this technique," I said. "It can't be the only palm technique out there."

"The Golden Circle still has its archives," Dex said. "We

can start there. I will speak to Professor Ziller. If anyone knows about the existence of this technique, it will be him."

"I will have our librarians research these techniques," Aria added. "Until then, please take this."

Aria gestured and materialized a short, black staff. I could tell it was made of Australian Buloke, because it resembled the door in the Randy Rump. Its entire surface was covered in runes which pulsed with a soft violet glow.

"What...is that?" Monty said with thinly veiled disgust. "Is that a—"

"Staff?" she finished. "Yes. It will act as a focus and allow you to access your energy until another solution can be found. This will prevent the aging, while its intact."

"A staff?" I asked. "Does that mean—?"

"Don't you dare," Monty said, warning me. "Don't even say it."

"Well, I may not be a mage," I said. "So I don't know much about these things, but if you can't access your magic without a staff"—a bright green flash blinded me, and Monty was gone—"doesn't that make you a wizard?"

Dex clapped me on the shoulder.

"You like to live dangerously, boy," he said, and turned to Aria. "Thank you for everything."

"And to you," Aria said. "We will offer every assistance we can."

Peaches blinked in next to me as Dex created another large green circle.

"We will find the answer," Dex said, rubbing Peaches behind the ears. "I will keep in touch. Let's go, boy."

I gave Aria a deep bow.

"Thank you," I said. "The blood lessons may have been a trap, but they saved my life."

"May the knowledge assist you in this new endeavor to restore Mage Montague."

"It will," I said, stepping into the circle. "We won't stop until we fix Monty's broken magic."

She bowed.

I returned the bow and the world flashed green, leaving the Cloisters behind.

THE END

AUTHOR NOTES

Thank you for reading this story and jumping into the world of Monty & Strong with me.

Disclaimer: The Author Notes are written at the very end of the writing process. This section is not seen by the ART or my amazing Jeditor—Audrey. Any typos or errors following this disclaimer are mine and mine alone.

Okay, I'll admit the ending on this one is skirting cliffhanger territory. I promise to get on the next one post haste. That was not the intention and at some point I wondered if we were ever going to get off the Hudson River.

RIP Mobula.

The story wanted to veer off in several directions, all of them exciting and explosive, but I made it a point to keep it on track. As it stands, this 50k book became a 64k book.

Do I learn? No. No, I do not.

Even with the wrangling, it ended the way it needed to end. The story itself is done, but the adventure continues and we need to fix Monty. After all, and there are some major enemies after them. When is the best time to attack a mage? When that mage is a wizard.

The next book is titled BROKEN MAGIC and picks up right after this one with a very cranky wizar <checks notes> mage...Mage Montague wielding a staff in new and creative ways to access his magic.

Will Simon remind him that only wizards use staves (yes, that is the plural, I checked) and risk getting bludgeoned by Monty's new staff? Yes, he certainly will.

This situation is different from the time Monty needed a focus (back in Homecoming). That time it was a result of a shift, this time, his access to magic is blocked. He needs to find a way around the block or begin to age, and as those of us who are less young know, after 200, it all starts to go downhill from there.

This story has many references to the number three. At first, the use was intentional, then it started multiplying almost with a mind of its own. Three is a fascinating number (numbers in general are amazing) and I could have gone overboard with references to triune, trinity, treble etc. Instead I settled for the Rule of Three (a real rule used mostly in speaking and literature) and worked with that as the context for all the other 'threes' in the story.

Simon is still poisoned, but now he has to make that poison work for him, there will be some mishaps in the future, some hilarious and some nerve wracking. Like everything else, Simon will learn as he does. In Broken Magic, some of the enemies that were lurking in the shadows, come into the light, sensing Monty's weakness and Simon's poisoned state.

They will be surprised at what they encounter. Really can't say more than that on that subject (no spoilers).

Verity isn't gone, but they are biding their time. Dealing with someone who can unleash a stormblood means they need to bring in heavy hitters. It's possible even the Tribunal will get involved, we will see. Expect to see more of Dex in the next few books. What didn't he do? Why is the Tribunal really upset with him? What is he doing with the Golden Circle? How are things going with the Morrigan?

Questions that he will answer (especially the one about the Morrigan), mostly in the next few books. You know how Dex can be. Also, prepare for a cameo from some of the Ten in the next book. Some of the members you know, but some have been waiting in the wings to make their appearance. They will have a chance in BROKEN MAGIC.

What else?

Oh, Simon has a necromantic blade. He needs to have a serious conversation with Michiko about where they are and Ebonsoul. He is going to meet up with a certain Night Warden trainee and she will help him open a door he needs opened. I mean, what are ciphers for if not unlocking the locked?

They still need to have a moment with a very unhappy Cecil. Even I don't know if they will survive that meeting. Cecil is not going to be pleased when he hears about the Mobula (RIP) and a new facet of the DAMNED will pay the Trio of Terror a visit, thanks to Ursula. All I know is that he goes by the name of the Actuary and strikes fear in all he meets.

There is so much more, but I don't want to spoil it for you (too much). Yes, more Midnight Echelon, especially Nan. A run in with a particular undead woman who is attracted to the energy of Ebonsoul (and Simon) and needs his help. Some Olga, plenty of Cece (how does Monty instruct when he can't access his magic easily?) and Peaches and Rags.

Will all this be in the next book? No, not all of it, but plenty of it will be, yes. I hope you hang in there with me as we find a way to get Monty access to his magic, deal with

Verity Agents, dodge Successors, and interact with angry goddesses of death bent on teaching Simon a lesson—no not that kind of lesson, I think.

Overall, I'm very excited for the next few books and I look forward to sharing the stories with you. Thank you so much for jumping into these stories with me (17 books WOW!). It's been an amazing ride, and I look forward to sharing them with you.

Never forget....Meat is Life!

Thank you again for jumping into this story with me!

SPECIAL MENTIONS

To Dolly: My rock, anchor, and inspiration. Thank you...always.

Larry & Tammy—The WOUF: Because even when you aren't there...you're there.

Orlando A. Sanchez
www.orlandoasanchez.com

Orlando has been writing ever since his teens when he was immersed in creating scenarios for playing Dungeons and Dragons with his friends every weekend.

The worlds of his books are urban settings with a twist of the paranormal lurking just behind the scenes and with generous doses of magic, martial arts, and mayhem.

He currently resides in Queens, NY with his wife and children.

BITTEN PEACHES PUBLISHING

Thanks for Reading

If you enjoyed this book, would you please **leave a review** at the site you purchased it from? It doesn't have to be long... just a line or two would be fantastic and it would really help me out.

Bitten Peaches Publishing offers more books by this author. From science fiction & fantasy to adventure & mystery, we bring the best stories for adults and kids alike.

www.BittenPeachesPublishing.com

More books by Orlando A. Sanchez

The Warriors of the Way

The Karashihan*•The Spiritual Warriors•The Ascendants•The Fallen Warrior•The Warrior Ascendant•The Master Warrior

John Kane

The Deepest Cut*•Blur

Sepia Blue
The Last Dance*•Rise of the
Night•Sisters•Nightmare•Nameless

Chronicles of the Modern Mystics
The Dark Flame•A Dream of Ashes

Montague & Strong Detective Agency Novels
Tombyards & Butterflies•Full Moon Howl•Blood is
Thicker•Silver Clouds Dirty Sky•Homecoming•Dragons &
Demigods•Bullets & Blades•Hell Hath No Fury•Reaping
Wind•The Golem•Dark Glass•Walking the
Razor•Requiem•Divine Intervention•Storm
Blood•Revenant•Blood Lessons

For those of you that prefer to listen to your books, you can find the entire M&S Series on Audiobooks.

Montague & Strong Detective Agency Audiobooks
The War Mage•No God is Safe•Tombyards & Butterflies•Full
Moon Howl•Blood is Thicker•Silver Clouds Dirty
Sky•Homecoming•Dragons & Demigods•Bullets &
Blades•Hell Hath No Fury•Reaping Wind•The Golem•Dark
Glass•Walking the Razor•Requiem•Divine Intervention

Montague & Strong Detective Agency Stories
No God is Safe•The Date•The War Mage•A Proper
Hellhound•The Perfect Cup•Saving Mr. K

Brew & Chew Adventures
Hellhound Blues

Night Warden Novels
Wander•ShadowStrut

Division 13
The Operative•The Magekiller

Blackjack Chronicles
The Dread Warlock

The Assassin's Apprentice
The Birth of Death

Gideon Shepherd Thrillers
Sheepdog

DAMNED
Aftermath

RULE OF THE COUNCIL
Blood Ascension•Blood Betrayal•Blood Rule

NYXIA WHITE
They Bite•They Rend•They Kill

IKER THE CLEANER
Iker the Unseen

Tales of the Gatekeepers
A Bullet Ballet

*Books denoted with an asterisk are **FREE** via my website
—www.orlandoasanchez.com

ART SHREDDERS

I want to take a moment to extend a special thanks to the ART SHREDDERS.

No book is the work of one person. I am fortunate enough to have an amazing team of advance readers and shredders.

Thank you for giving of your time and keen eyes to provide notes, insights, answers to the questions, and corrections (dealing wonderfully with my extreme dreaded comma allergy). You help make every book and story go from good to great. Each and every one of you helped make this book fantastic, and I couldn't do this without each of you.

THANK YOU

ART SHREDDERS

Amber, Anne Morando, Audrey Cienki
   Beverly Collie
   Carrie Anne O'Leary, Cat, Chris Christman II, Colleen Taylor

Davina Noble, Dawn McQueen Mortimer, Denise King, Desmond Auer, Diana Gray, Dolly Sanchez, Donna Young Hatridge

Hal Bass

Jasmine Breeden, Jasmine Davis, Jeanette Auer, Jen Cooper, Jim Maguire, John Fauver, Joy Kiili, Joy Ollier, Julie Peckett

Karen Hollyhead

Larry Diaz Tushman, Laura Tallman I

Malcolm Robertson, Marcia Campbell, Mari De Valerio, Maryelaine Eckerle-Foster, Melissa Miller, Melody DeLoach, Michelle Blue

Paige Guido, Penny Campbell-Myhill

RC Battels, Rene Corrie, Rob Farnham

Sara Mason Branson, Sean Trout, Sondra Massey, Stacey Stein, Susie Johnson

Tami Cowles, Tanya Anderson, Ted Camer, Terri Adkisson

Vikki Brannagan

Wanda Corder-Jones, Wendy Schindler

ACKNOWLEDGEMENTS

With each book, I realize that every time I learn something about this craft, it highlights so many things I still have to learn. Each book, each creative expression, has a large group of people behind it.

This book is no different.

Even though you see one name on the cover, it is with the knowledge that I am standing on the shoulders of the literary giants that informed my youth, and am supported by my generous readers who give of their time to jump into the adventures of my overactive imagination.

I would like to take a moment to express my most sincere thanks:

To Dolly: My wife and greatest support. You make all this possible each and every day. You keep me grounded when I get lost in the forest of ideas. Thank you for asking the right questions when needed, and listening intently when I go off on tangents. Thank you for who you are and the space you create—I love you.

To my Tribe: You are the reason I have stories to tell. You cannot possibly fathom how much and how deeply I love you all.

To Lee: Because you were the first reader I ever had. I love you, sis.

To the Logsdon Family: The words *thank you* are insufficient to describe the gratitude in my heart for each of you. JL, your support always demands I bring my best, my A-game, and produce the best story I can. Both you and Lorelei (my Uber Jeditor) and now, Audrey, are the reason I am where I am today. My thank you for the notes, challenges, corrections, advice, and laughter. Your patience is truly infinite. *Arigato-gozaimasu.*

To The Montague & Strong Case Files Group—AKA The MoB (Mages of Badassery): When I wrote T&B there were fifty-five members in The MoB. As of this release, there are over one thousand four hundred members in the MoB. I am honored to be able to call you my MoB Family. Thank you for being part of this group and M&S.

You make this possible. **THANK YOU.**

To the ever-vigilant PACK: You help make the MoB...the MoB. Keeping it a safe place for us to share and just...be. Thank you for your selfless vigilance. You truly are the Sentries of Sanity.

Chris Christman II: A real-life technomancer who makes the **MoBTV LIVEvents +Kaffeeklatsch** on YouTube amazing. Thank you for your tireless work and wisdom. Everything is connected...you totally rock!

To the WTA—The Incorrigibles: JL, Ben Z. Eric QK., S.S., and Noah.

They sound like a bunch of badass misfits, because they are. My exposure to the deranged and deviant brain trust you all represent helped me be the author I am today. I have officially gone to the *dark side* thanks to all of you. I humbly give you my thanks, and...it's all your fault.

To my fellow Indie Authors, specifically the tribe at 20books to 50k: Thank you for creating a space where authors can feel listened to, and encouraged to continue on this path. A rising tide lifts all the ships indeed.

To The English Advisory: Aaron, Penny, Carrie, Davina, and all of the UK MoB. For all things English...thank you.

To DEATH WISH COFFEE: This book (and every book I write) has been fueled by generous amounts of the only coffee on the planet (and in space) strong enough to power my very twisted imagination. Is there any other coffee that can compare? I think not. DEATHWISH—thank you!

To Deranged Doctor Design: Kim, Darja, Tanja, Jovana, and Milo (Designer Extraordinaire).

If you've seen the covers of my books and been amazed, you can thank the very talented and gifted creative team at DDD. They take the rough ideas I give them, and produce incredible covers that continue to surprise and amaze me. Each time, I find myself striving to write a story worthy of the covers they produce. DDD, you embody professionalism and creativity. Thank you for the great service and spectacular covers. **YOU GUYS RULE!**

To you, the reader: I was always taught to save the best for last. I write these stories for **you**. Thank you for jumping down the rabbit holes of ***what if?*** with me. You are the reason I write the stories I do.

You keep reading...I'll keep writing.

Thank you for your support and encouragement.

CONTACT ME

I really do appreciate your feedback. You can let me know
what you thought of the story by emailing me at:
orlando@orlandoasanchez.com

To get **FREE** stories please visit my page at:
www.orlandoasanchez.com

For more information on the M&S World...come join the
MoB Family on Facebook!
You can find us at:
Montague & Strong Case Files

Visit our online M&S World Swag Store located at:
Emandes

You can follow me on Twitter at:
@AuthorOSanchez

Please follow our amazing instagram page at:
bittenpeaches

Follow us on Patreon at:
BittenPeachesPublishing

If you enjoyed the book, **please leave a review**. Reviews help the book, and also help other readers find good stories to read.
THANK YOU!

Thanks for Reading
If you enjoyed this book, would you **please leave a review** at the site you purchased it from? It doesn't have to be a book report... just a line or two would be fantastic and it would really help us out!

Printed in Great Britain
by Amazon